I SPY . . .

Television experimenter Curtis Drew sets out to combine the X-ray with television to aid surgery. However, he discovers instead 'pure' television — invisible 'Z-rays' which have the potential to receive and record any situation — anywhere. Nothing is private any more. Immoral acts, and hidden crimes can all be exposed. The 'Z-ray' could benefit humanity, yet to Drew it opens up more lucrative possibilities. He becomes a scientific 'Peeping Tom' and blackmailer, but when murder results, Scotland Yard becomes interested . . .

JOHN RUSSELL FEARN

---◆---

I SPY . . .

Complete and Unabridged

LINFORD
Leicester

First published in Great Britain

First Linford Edition
published 2008

British Library CIP Data

Fearn, John Russell, *1908 – 1960*
 I spy.—Large print ed.—
 Linford mystery library
 1. Exortion—Fiction 2. Electronic surveillance—
 Fiction 3. Detective and mystery stories
 4. Large type books
 I. Title
 823.9'12 [F]

 ISBN 978–1–84782–491–2

Published by
F. A. Thorpe (Publishing)
Anstey, Leicestershire

Set by Words & Graphics Ltd.
Anstey, Leicestershire
Printed and bound in Great Britain by
T. J. International Ltd., Padstow, Cornwall

This book is printed on acid-free paper

1

The Z-ray

Just as in the twentieth century there existed many thousands of 'ham' radio engineers who spent most of their spare time transmitting amateur radio programs and discussing various radio topics with each other, sometimes at opposite ends of the world, so in the next century there sprang up a new order of fanatics. In the main these young men and women were concerned with the transmission of color television, and were sending each other endless scenes in three dimensions which did not in any way interfere with the normal television bands.

Curtis Drew however, a brilliant television engineer, was not by any means satisfied with the simple exchange of the three-dimensional projections across intervening miles. He wanted a great deal more — preferably something that would finally turn him in a great deal of money. As yet he was only young — thirty — and he felt that with the undoubted skill he possessed something worthwhile should be made to arise from this constant spare-time devotion to an extremely absorbing hobby.

Curtis Drew was not alone in his belief. By his side there constantly worked his sister Christine, and his friend since College days, Dick Englefield. All three of them were more or less as 'crazy' as each other, but all three had this one singleness of purpose — that they ought to be able to eventually rake in some kind of financial return for the expenditure of energy and cash which their absorbing hobby demanded.

It was Christine who finally developed a quite logical idea. Her normal occupation was on the clerical side of one of the city's biggest hospitals. In this capacity she had been enabled to see many of the private reports submitted by surgeons and others of the medical fraternity for recording purposes, and she had not been slow to appreciate that even in these scientific days there were many barriers in the way of supreme surgical achievement. And it was from this that her idea had undoubtedly stemmed.

'Why,' she asked her brother, when the idea had fully matured, 'do you not convert television processes to the more important field of surgery? By that I mean devise some process by which surgeons may be enabled to see clearly inside a human body. See exactly what is wrong with it, and therefore know what needs doing to repair it. I know there are X-rays, sound scans and those kinds of devices, but nowadays even those are very antiquated. There are micro cameras that can be inserted into the body, of course, but there are many occasions when they cannot be used — with serious injuries, for instance. It seems to me there ought to be some process by which a surgeon should be able to see an interior organ, and have it reflected with perfect clarity on to some kind of screen, whereby he can assess in absolute detail just what is needed to put it right. In much the same fashion as an engineer is enabled to study the insides of metals and the strains and stresses that they will take, all by scientific equipment. By that means bridges and other engineering constructions are absolutely safe — but no such thing seems to exist to help the surgeon.'

There was no gainsaying the fact that the idea was an extremely good one and Curtis Drew was not slow either in seeing the financial possibilities that might accrue from such an invention, if only he could perfect it. Immediately he went to work to study all the processes of television, both on the transmission and the dimensional side, and from it there finally emerged what he was pleased to call his Z-ray. Up to this point he had not explained either to his sister or Dick Englefield what he was trying to do. They Had merely continued with their ordinary television transmissions and left Curtis to his own devices. But finally there came the day when, with proud triumph in his voice, Curtis announced that he had perfected his extraordinary invention.

'I don't see why you couldn't have told us something about it,' Christine objected, on the evening that he had set apart for his demonstration. 'After all, we're in this up to the neck as much as you are.'

'To a certain extent, Chris,' Curtis corrected. 'This is entirely my own invention when you've said and done all — so I'm afraid I don't see quite eye to eye with the 'all of us' angle.'

Christine gave Dick Englefield a glance. Dick was big, burly — good-humored to a degree — and for that matter Christine too was a girl of extremely equable temperament, except when dealing with her brother. She knew better than anybody else his immense, overriding ambition and she also knew that if he ever did get his hands on a source of extreme power there would be no stopping him. She and Curtis Drew were both dark and extremely intelligent, but whereas Christine had a definite womanly sweetness about her, there was in Curtis a brusqueness of style and in acidity of tongue which made of him by no means an easy man to understand.

'The one-for-all and all-for-one technique applies only to the television department,' he said after a moment or two. 'This stunt, if it works, is entirely mine. Now I'd better give you an outline of what I've been doing all these weeks. Later on, if I can, I'll try and give you a demonstration.'

'Why do you say 'if you can'?' Dick Englefield asked, in surprise. 'Haven't you worked on the thing long enough to know whether it operates or not?'

'I'm perfectly sure that it will operate, but so far I have been concerned mainly with the mechanics and haven't yet experimented on a living creature to see if it functions in the way I believe it should do. To get back to the point, however — the basis of my Z-ray came into being when I was studying, quite by chance, a drawing of a lunar eclipse. You are both aware that during a lunar eclipse there are two shadows, the false shadow and the true — better known in technical language as the penumbra and umbra. The penumbra is the false shadow cast by the moon and the umbra is the real shadow of the eclipse itself. In other words the penumbra is the area of diffusion which exists outside the true shadow cone.'

'I quite fail to see,' Christine remarked, 'how the penumbra-umbra lunar shadow could give you the basis of your idea. It isn't even related to radiant transmission in any way.'

'As to that,' Curtis answered, 'it depends what kind of a mind you've got and how far you can visualize the ultimate outcome of a scientific basis. Now for the sake of our little illustration, let us imagine that the umbra, or true shadow, is the Z-ray that my apparatus will send forth. Clear, so far?'

Christine and Dick Englefield both nodded together.

'Very well. This Z-ray beam is what one might call an exciter radiation. When it strikes an object, even if that object be within another object, it energizes the light photons which it — the Z-ray — carries with it on its journey to the object in question. That is based on the principle of a luminous object, shining by

7

reason of the fact that during the daylight hours it has absorbed a great quantity of light photons, which it reradiates in the darkness. So this Z-ray strikes our object and immediately our object is lighted up. Your immediate reply to that will be that lighting up an object inside another object is of no use at all because it cannot be seen — and my reply would be, how right you are!

'I very soon appreciated this fact when I devised the Z-ray. It immediately became obvious that something more was needed. It was then that I hit upon the idea of an electronic reflecting beam. This beam acts on the principle of a mirror reflecting a light. For instance, if you reflect a light from a mirror it strikes the point required and is then reflected back again at exactly the same angle as it is transmitted. Forming, in other words, a V-shaped design.

'This electronic beam, then, operates at the same time as the Z-ray and travels to the same object. This electronic beam also has another property by which it limits the extent to which the Z-ray can travel, thereby making it capable of being focused at any particular point, be it near or far. What happens is — the electronic beam decides what the objective is to be — or at least I decide it for it — and when it reaches that objective it forms an invisible barrier in the ether, which, of course, exists everywhere and is the transmitter of all radiations. That means that when the Z-ray strikes this barrier in the ether — which is also the pre-determined objective — it cannot go any further; it must illuminate that one particular point that the electronic beam has in focus.

'Now it is obviously logical that the reflection from the electronic beam must go somewhere. You cannot stop a thing dead or have it absorbed or re-dissipated. Just as in the case of a mirror you cannot reflect a light and not expect it to go anywhere. It is immediately re-distributed in various light waves from the original source. So it is with this electronic beam. When it strikes the objective it is immediately reflected back again at exactly the same angle at which it was projected, forming again a perfect V-shape in absolutely straight lines. So then our whole construction looks rather like an electronic beam being a 'V', that is transmission point, point of incidence, and point of reception — the transmission and reception points forming the two top points of the V, and the objective forming the base of the V, whilst the Z-ray goes straight down the centre and strikes the bottom point of the V . . . '

'I think,' Christine said, pondering, 'that I begin to grasp what you mean. You transmit the electronic and Z-rays simultaneously and when the objective is reached it is energized into being illuminated, and the reflecting electronic beam directs the image up the 'reflection' path — or in other words the opposite arm of the V, back to the receiving point. Is that what you mean?'

'That's it,' Curtis assented, nodding. With that he turned aside to the apparatus nearby and proceeded to indicate it. With interest Christine and Dick Englefield studied the equipment. They had of course seen it in the process of construction during the past weeks, but this was the first time that they had had the opportunity of seeing it in its finished state.

Altogether it comprised three separate sets of equipment. On the left stood the complicated receiving apparatus, and two feet away from it in the center was the transmitter for the Z-ray, whilst two feet further away on the right was the transmitter for the electronic beam. The transmitter and receiver for the electronic beam were turned slightly inwards on their universal mountings, whilst the Z-ray transmitter faced exactly frontward. All three were supported on heavily greased double rails which made them capable of being pushed closer together or spread wider apart, by which means it was assumed that Curtis would be able to maintain full control over them as he examined whatever objective he had in mind.

'Pretty cumbersome stuff,' was Dick Englefield's comment after a while, and Curtis gave him a glance.

'No more cumbersome than the X-ray

equipment used in modern laboratories and hospitals. The main factor in the basis of this apparatus is that the nearer the objective, the sharper the inward convergence of the transmitter and receiver for the electronic beam. However, as near as I have been able to work it out in mathematics, it should be possible to get a correct convergence on an object three feet away, and if what I believe of this apparatus is true it should mean that an exact picture of anything internal will be reflected up the electronic beam to the screen which you see on the receiver there. Incidentally, as in television or radio, the image picked up is entirely electronic and the necessary transformers rebuild it back into its original material form, if I may call it such.'

'There's one point I don't quite get,' Christine remarked, as she went round the back of the equipment and pondered its infinite complication, 'and that is how you control this Z-ray so that it can go through one solid and yet stop it short at another one. Surely for that kind of work

12

it must have many of the properties of the X-ray?'

'Definitely it has,' Curtis assented. 'As to why it can pass through one solid and yet be stopped by another, I thought I had made it clear when I said that the electronic beam is the means by which the Z-ray is limited in its distance. Electronic beams take no cognizance of solids whatever; they simply operate upon ether. Therefore, if our objective — for example's sake — be a hundred feet away, I set the electronic beam for one hundred feet. At the same time I also put in operation the equipment which gives me the exact angle at which the transmitter must be turned to cover that one hundred feet and make certain that the Z-ray will also reach the objective at the exact point.

'Now, when that electronic beam has travelled the hundred feet it will set up a barrier in the ether through which the Z-ray cannot pass. At that hundred-foot distance the Z-ray excites the light photons of the object decided upon, and the electronic beam, reflecting itself up the other arm of the beam, carries the image which the Z-ray has illuminated, and the finished result appears on the screen there. It is all a matter of electronics and etheric reflections. A lot of it is used in television today and this is merely a modification of the basic principles.

'The Z-ray, if it were not blocked by this etheric barrier set up by the electronic beam, would go on travelling forever, or at least something approaching that. What I mean is, it goes straight through all solids and having got power enough it would finally leave the Earth altogether in a straight line and go right out into outer space. Nothing can stop its penetrating qualities except the ether barrier which the electronic beam instantly creates.'

'Well,' Dick Englefield said, scratching the back of his head, 'I have to admit that it's a darned good idea, even though I only half understand it. How about a demonstration?'

Curtis nodded promptly. 'That is exactly the reason why I asked you and Sis to be here early tonight. To get the best results we obviously need to look inside a living object, and I cannot use myself as the subject — though I would willingly do so — because I have to operate the mechanism. So it is up to either you or Sis to be a volunteer. If Sis were my brother instead of my sister I'd tell her to get on with the job, or else! But since she's a woman,' Curtis grinned, 'she may not be quite so willing to have this beam start putting a floodlight inside her.'

Christine shrugged. 'I haven't the least objection.'

'I'll do it,' Dick Englefield volunteered, 'mainly for the simple reason that you might be able to tell me why I keep getting pains in the chest just lately. Either it's indigestion or else a bad heart — I don't know which — so perhaps this Z-ray apparatus of yours might be able to make the thing clear. Where do I stand?'

Curtis indicated the square metal plate directly in front of the Z-ray apparatus, at a distance of about two feet from it. Dick lounged across to it, stood in position, and then waited.

'Just so long as I'm not supposed to

strip as well, I'm quite happy,' he commented, with a wry smile.

'No need for that,' Curtis told him, busy with the switchboard. 'Just stand as you are and the Z-ray will penetrate clothes, bone, flesh, and all the lot. You won't feel anything at all, not even a suggestion of warmth, yet on the screen here there should be an exact reflection of everything the Z-ray is looking at.'

Christine sat down slowly and waited, definitely absorbed by this miracle that her brother's keen mind had devised. Certainly she had never suspected when she had mentioned the medical angle that such an abstrusely brilliant contrivance would have emerged. Then the small generator began to hum and her interest immediately began to liven. She smiled across at Dick as he saluted solemnly and watched the blunt-nosed snout of the Z-ray equipment facing directly at him. Curtis, for his part, was busy with the computer. This was linked to the apparatus that gave him the necessary angles and positions for the electronic transmitter and receiver. At last he was ready and gave Dick an enquiring glance.

'There's just one thing,' Dick said, slowly, before he gave acquiescence to start.

'Well?' Curtis looked irritated for he had just been about to switch the apparatus into operation.

'How do we all stand if this thing turns out to be a success?' Dick enquired. 'You have invented it, and I am the guinea pig. Though I don't doubt that you've worked this thing out to the last scientific decimal, there does remain the possibility that something might go wrong and I might get bumped off — therefore it may be considered that I'm taking a risk with my life and I feel that it entitles me to a certain amount of financial profit if the invention should prove to be successful. For there's no doubt that if it is the medical world will snap it up in a moment and the reimbursement for such a device would undoubtedly be considerable. You can't blame me for acting as a businessman before you put the experiment into full swing.'

Curtis shrugged. 'All right, if that's the

way you feel about it. I don't blame you, of course; in your position I would probably do the same thing. I suggest that if the thing is worthwhile and does all that I think it will — that we split whatever is likely to accrue from it in three directions. Yourself, and of course, Christine, and myself. How's that?'

'Sounds fair enough,' Christine admitted, but she did not add that she would have liked it in writing. Knowing her brother as well as she did she was not inclined to take him on the same face value as Dick was.

'That weighty matter being settled,' Curtis remarked dryly, 'are we ready to commence?'

Dick nodded. 'Shoot, father, I am not afraid.'

With that Curtis jammed home the master switch that transferred the power to the electronic transmitter and also the Z-ray projector. Nothing was visibly emanating from either instrument, and as far as Dick himself was concerned he just stood unconcernedly, hands pushed in the pockets of his loose sports jacket as he waited for something to happen. Christine and her brother at the front of the apparatus concentrated their attention on the main screen fitted to the electronic receiver.

Seconds passed and nothing happened. The apparatus droned on steadily and as the screen still remained blank — or rather it was filled with a puzzling mass of waving lines — Curtis began to show the first signs of obvious bafflement. He began a quick checking of the apparatus, studying the switches and inspecting meters, making sure that everything was exactly as it should be. Even so nothing appeared on the screen as the seconds lengthened into a minute and then two minutes. Dick, watching, could easily tell that something was the matter and he raised his eyebrows enquiringly.

'What's the trouble?' he enquired. 'Aren't you getting my wavelengths?'

Curtis gave him a brief glance. 'Frankly I just can't understand it. There ought to be a complete recording here, yet there isn't a single sign of anything at all. I must have slipped up badly somewhere, but for the life of me I can't imagine where it can be.'

'All that trouble for nothing,' Dick sighed; relaxing and coming away from the transmission plate. 'Not that I'm finding any fault with your scientific abilities, Curt, because I know only too well what you can do. Evidently the set-up on paper is a very different thing when you start to do it in practice. Want me to help you have a look and see if we can check what's the matter with it?'

Curtis shook his head briefly. 'No thanks, I can handle this entirely by myself. You and Chris go back to your television stuff and leave me to puzzle out what's gone wrong here.'

Accustomed to his abrupt manner when annoyed or puzzled neither Dick nor Christine took umbrage at Curtis' manner. They wandered across to the television equipment and Christine settled herself. She seemed quite prepared to carry on with their normal amateur television broadcasts, but plainly Dick was not that way inclined. The puzzle of the new-fangled apparatus which had not functioned as it should was still on his mind. He went back to where Curtis was standing looking at the meters intently.

The power was still running and, as far as Dick could tell, the apparatus was therefore still in action.

'I don't know anything about the equipment,' Dick said, in a half-apologetic voice, 'but are you sure that you've got the distance and everything else exactly right? I imagine an apparatus as sensitive as this will have to be correct to within a thirty-second of an inch to make it work in the way that you hope.'

'Is that meant to imply that I don't know what I'm doing?' Curtis asked, glancing at him coldly.

'No, nothing like that, I'm just trying to be helpful, and you don't have to take that attitude either!'

Just for a moment an angry glint smouldered in Dick's blue eyes then it died away again as Curtis gave a rueful smile.

'Sorry,' he apologized, clapping Dick on the shoulders. 'I'm too darned worried to choose my words carefully. I was convinced I'd got this thing exactly right, yet all we can get on the screen is an electronic translation of the transmission itself, which, of course, is absolutely pointless.'

Dick nodded and took a few paces forward to examine the equipment. He did not notice as he moved that his foot caught under one of the many thick cables snaking about the laboratory floor. He only realized what he had done when he stumbled forward and accidentally caught the electronic transmitter with his shoulder. Immediately the heavy apparatus swung through a quarter circle on its universal mountings. Since it was automatically geared to the receiver, the receiver also moved inwards by a quarter of a turn, which meant that the original angle that had been set was now hopelessly awry.

'For God's sake take care of what you're doing,' Curtis cried in anger. 'Next thing we know you'll knock the whole damned apparatus to bits! Why can't you — '

Curtis broke off in mid-sentence, his

eyes fixed on the screen and his expression one of breathless wonder. Dick slowly straightened up and when he too saw what was on the screen he gave a gasp of amazement and then stared fixedly. Christine, noting the sudden silence of the two men, glanced over her shoulder, rose to her feet, and came across to where they were standing.

In silent amazement all three of them watched the scene depicted on the receiving end of the electronic apparatus. It depicted some nameless main street, which could have been anywhere, and it was plainly evening. Overhead were the normal high-powered daylight tubes used in these days on all main traffic ways, and on either side of the street were the brightly lighted windows of shops, which, though closed, were still displaying their wares. Along the pavements men and women jostled or passed each other, or stopped to do some window gazing, apparently walking right into the camera range then melting away as they passed beyond focus of the uncanny instrument. But where was this place? And why in the name of wonder had it suddenly appeared on this screen, which was supposed to be designed for close range examination?

'Why,' Christine exclaimed, 'this is about the most wonderful television effect I have ever seen! It isn't three-dimensional I know, but it is at least absolutely acid-clear in its imagery, and there isn't a trace of interference either!'

'I can see that,' Curtis told her, irritably, 'but the point is, what the devil location have we happened upon? Can you read the names on those shops? Are they British or foreign or what?'

This led them to peer more closely at the rock-steady scene displayed before them. By degrees they managed to discover that the names over the shops were indeed quite English. There were such names as 'Sanderson', 'Browning', 'Richards & Son'. Anything more English in the way of surnames could hardly be imagined, and apparently there were confectioners, clothiers, furniture dealers, costumiers, and all the ordinary trades which grace the main streets of any town, anywhere.

As his wonder subsided, Curtis turned quickly to the apparatus and inspected the displays that were connected with the transmitter-receiver system.

'This doesn't tell us much,' he commented, as Christine and Dick moved to his side. 'You see this pointer arrangement here which moves along this graduated scale? The idea of it is that it gives me the exact distance from one to six feet, but in this instance, with you happening to catch the transmitter as you did, Dick, the pointer has been swung right off the edge of the scale and is just hanging in mid-air so I don't know exactly where the transmitter is pointing.'

'It's perfectly obvious where it's pointing,' Christine said. 'By some inexplicable fluke the apparatus is picking up a steady scene from a town somewhere. In this laboratory here we're on the outskirts of London, so the best guess is that we're picking up something in the middle of London.'

There was silence for a moment then Dick snapped his fingers.

'Tell you what! That's a main street

— that's perfectly plain — so before long there ought to be a 'bus service or something and if we can read the name on the bus as it goes past we might be able to figure out what we're looking at!'

The commonsense of this observation was plain so they returned to the screen to see what happened next. As before they could not help but be fascinated by the uncanny clarity of the picture they were viewing, insofar that as distinct from normal flat and three-dimensional television, this particular product had an intense clearness and absolute steadiness which made it just as though they were looking through an ordinary clear glass window upon the actual scene itself. Curtis was definitely the most puzzled of the three because he knew — or fancied he knew — the limitations of his apparatus. Then suddenly Dick gave a sudden exclamation.

'Here's a bus! Keep your eyes skinned, both of you!'

There was no need for the instruction. Christine, Curtis and Dick himself all watched intently as the 'bus moved with commendable slowness into the picture and stopped to drop a couple of passengers. This particular occurrence made it perfectly easy to read the pin-sharp name on the front of the 'bus. It said 'Halgate Road' and as it moved on again into the range of the receiving beam the side of the bus came momentarily into view with the name of the appropriate Corporation written upon it. All three watchers could not help but gasp as they read 'Leicester County Council.'

'But this is absolutely ridiculous!' Dick exclaimed in amazement. 'Why, Leicester is over a hundred miles away from here! It just isn't possible for us to have picked up something from there. The only answer is that there is some kind of a joke going on here, perhaps engineered by some of our fellow television hams who somehow managed to contact us.'

But even as he talked he knew how utterly impossible his solution was. Not that Curtis was listening for a moment, for he had again returned to the apparatus and was contemplating it with an almost feverish intensity. Finally he reached out his hand to one of the countless controlling knobs and gave it a very slight turn. The effect of this was to alter the picture on the screen so that the street slewed out of view, and instead there came into sight the enormous façade of a theatre. As the beam came to rest it picked up the figures of men and women entering the brightly lighted foyer.

'What did you do then?' Christine asked quickly, and for a moment Curtis took his attention from the dials to glance towards her.

'All I did was slightly change the range which normally would have moved us about an eighth of an inch; instead it seems to have shifted us ten or twenty feet across the street. Which,' he went on, thinking, 'gives us something of a clue. It looks to me as though by the merest chance we've happened on to the most extraordinary development of television ever discovered.'

Neither Christine nor Dick answered: they were too absorbed in watching the view-screen, but as Curtis closed the master switch the picture faded and the screen became blank.

'Sorry,' he apologized, laconically, 'but we've more important things to do than just gaze at that. I begin to see what has happened, and I will try to explain it as well as I can . . . Here, sit down while I try and make the details clear to you.'

The three seated themselves at the small laboratory table, and for a moment or two Curtis considered, then removing a pencil from his overall pocket he laid it on the center of the table.

'If I turn this pencil so,' he explained, and suited the action to the word by rotating the pointed end in a semi-circle whilst he kept the other end perfectly stationary with his finger upon it, 'we can see that while the top end of the pencil only moves a distance of perhaps a quarter of an inch, the point of the pencil covers a distance of four or five inches. That of course is quite normal in the law of angles and the length appertaining thereto. The further away the end of an object like this is from its fulcrum, the wider the angles through which it passes.

'What seems to have happened in this

29

instance is that all unwittingly we have happened on a form of television which is absolutely unique. I had originally planned the apparatus for very close range work — such as the examination of the internal workings of animals and human beings and so forth — but this is something infinitely greater and much more fascinating! Leicester, of course, being over a hundred miles away, is well below our horizon point, and yet we get a perfectly clear picture. That means that the Z-ray we're generating has passed through all solids and simply traveled in an absolutely straight line and has been stopped by the electronic mated radiation that always goes with it.

'When you hit the transmitter, Dick, you must have knocked the pointer to an exceptionally wide angle which caused the narrow focus I had arranged, when I was examining you, to be suddenly spread out to almost its widest extent. This meant that instead of covering a few feet, the beam has traveled over a hundred miles in a perfectly straight line. When it hit the blockage of ether caused by the electronic radiation, it reflected back the scene at which it had been stopped, which apparently is one of the main streets in Leicester. And judging by the voltage and the output, the apparatus is quite capable of reaching ten, twenty, and even fifty times further than this without seriously affecting its actual power output.'

Something seemed to suddenly occur to Christine.

'Might that not account for the fact, Curt, that you were not able to get a close-range reading as you had expected? As I see it, this apparatus relies for its efficiency upon the foci of the electronic vibration and the Z-ray absolutely synchronizing at the point of impingement. Perhaps the distance of only a few feet was so small that it couldn't possibly accommodate itself to it, but when it was accidentally widened in its angle it picked up the scene with perfect ease and reproduced what it saw on that screen!'

'Yes, that's more than reasonably possible,' Curtis agreed, getting to his feet again. 'What I am anxious to do is to find out if this thing really is some new form of long distance television. If so there are very few limits one can set upon it. Anyway, let's see what we can do . . . '

2

Blackmail

Again Curtis switched on the apparatus and Christine and Dick stood aside whilst he operated the controls. It was plain from his expression that he was completely in the dark as to what he was doing because the pointer control which normally handled the distance which the twin beams would travel was completely out of commission, there being no graded scale upon which it could operate.

Yet as Curtis moved it about — practically in mid-air — the scenes on the television screen changed constantly and even jumped when he gave the pointer a jerk, showing that the electronic beam had widened its influence and allowed the Z-ray to leap forward to another point until it again hit the barrier in the ether which the electronic radiations set up.

By this means the Z-ray literally

travelled in leaps and bounds in a northerly direction, merely because that happened to be the direction that the televisor was facing. But there was no doubt as that mysterious influence fled across the night-covered British Isles that they were receiving scenes from towns and cities and hamlets, each one more northerly than its predecessor. By a little maneuvering Curtis was quite easily able to pick up the center of Manchester, and from there by a mere movement on the still not properly connected pointer, he managed to leap forward again as far as Glasgow and then upwards into the Scottish Highlands. Here, he paused for a moment and put out the laboratory lights. Upon the screen were hung a view of the Scottish mountains and glens, still and silent under a starlit sky, with here and there a spot of light which denoted perhaps a cottage.

'It's uncanny,' Christine whispered, nearly awestruck. 'Why, Curt, this is nothing more or less than an ubiquitous eye! Apparently it can go everywhere and see everything — at least as far as this country goes. Do you suppose that you can get the range even greater than that?'

'No doubt about it,' Curtis cried, in delight. It was amazing the transformation which had come to him in the last hour of roaming with his incredible Z-ray. With every scene that had appeared on the screen he had grasped more clearly the almost inconceivable possibilities of the accidental discovery that had been made.

'How about some fine focus?' Dick asked, turning from contemplating the view of the darkened hills of Scotland. 'By that I mean can you alter it so that you can say pick up one person instead of having to wander over wide areas and getting this panorama type of view?'

'The fine focus business is the easiest job in the world,' Curtis replied. 'Best thing we can do is return to one of the cities — say Glasgow — and — '

'No, wait a minute,' Christine cut in. 'Look at that screen there! There are tiny spots of light, which must belong to dwellings of some kind. Can you fine focus one of them and see what lies behind the light, or maybe the source of the light itself?'

Curtis nodded. 'I think I can. I may be a bit rocky on the manoeuvering side of the job, since this is the first experiment, but anyway I'll have a try.'

He turned back to the apparatus and once again controlled the dozens of small, calibrated knobs that governed the extraordinary equipment. After some wavering the lowest spot of light on the screen began to rise forward out of the dark just as though it were some dim headlight on a motorcar. The effect in the darkened laboratory was positively uncanny, and Dick and Christine stood beside each other and watched in fascination as the light came nearer and nearer swallowing up the darkened mountain country in which it lay. Presently it was transformed from a mere vague illumination into the obvious outline of a small window in a dimly visible white cottage. But the astounding ray did not stop here; apparently it went clean through the window into the interior of a small, parlor-type of room.

There was a sudden click as Curtis made an adjustment and the sensation of traveling forward abruptly stopped. The view became steady on this remote room in the Scottish Highlands, and in dead silence the trio looked at a solitary old man seated at a hardwood table chewing at a supper, which looked to be bread and cheese, and reading a newspaper at the same time. Beside him, quite distinct in the light of the oil-lamp by which he was reading, there sat an extremely woolly sheep-dog. Casting reflections in the background were plates and ornaments on a tall dresser and from other parts of the room the oil-lamp was reflected from modest but nonetheless comfortable furniture. In the grate a cheerful fire was burning brightly.

'This is absolute wizardry!' Dick exclaimed finally. 'We're just eavesdropping on this old man in the far Scottish Highlands, and he hasn't the remotest idea that we're looking at him! No transmitter at the other end, no anything! This is television as it should be!'

'There is a transmitter at the other

end,' Curtis corrected, 'but not of the type that we understand. It is simply caused by a barrier in the ether, the excitation of light photons at that barrier by the Z-ray, and the reflection of those excited light photons back along the electronic beam to the receiving screen there. And I think,' he added after a moment or two, 'that I can get an even better focus than this. I'll just try anyhow . . . '

He moved back to the equipment and buried himself again at the controls until very gradually the full view of the room was slowly supplanted by the face of the old man. He appeared to be a shepherd, and as the equipment was even more finely focused his head and shoulders and rugged old face gradually moved up into view until it finally filled the whole of the screen. That was the uncanny part about it. The abstracted look in his eyes as he read the newspaper, the steady movement of his jaws as he chewed his simple bread and cheese, the oil light casting on the ruggedness of his grand old face, etching out every line and wrinkle with a clarity never known or seen before either in television or film camera work. This was a transmission of the actual object by the most perfect reproducing system possible — namely, the translation of the actual light waves themselves into a flawless rendering of the original subject.

'It's a funny thing,' Christine said presently, glancing at her brother, 'but some of the greatest inventions the world has ever known have come about by accident, and it begins to look as though this is another case of it! You set out to invent a surgical instrument that would penetrate the outer covering of a human being or an animal, and instead Dick falling over a wire has brought into being the most perfect television method ever known! Used in the right way it can be of colossal value and used in the wrong way it could bring civilization down like a pack of cards!'

'Yes,' Curtis agreed, thinking deeply, 'how right you are!'

'Reverting to the scientific side,' Dick said, after a moment or two, 'Scotland is obviously a tremendous distance below the horizon as seen from London. Have you juggled this Z-ray round at all or is it still just travelling in a straight line which includes Scotland in its journey?'

'No,' Curtis answered. 'I've altered its angle as I've progressed. Lifting it or lowering it according to whatever place I want. There's no limit to what it can do, but since we've got this far there's no reason why we shouldn't get further. I propose to see just how far this thing can go. Stand by while we see what limits it has — if any.'

He turned back to the apparatus and with the laboratory itself being in darkness he was only visible as a dim silhouette working intently on the spot-lighted switchboard. Dick and Christine for their part drew up chairs and settled comfortably before the screen, watching as the flawless close-up of the Scottish shepherd gradually faded away and was replaced by a long-range vision of a continent of ice and snow, silent and deserted under the stars. In the distance were the fantastic curtains of the aurora borealis.

'That,' came Curtis' voice, dryly, out of the gloom, 'is a modern version of 'furthest north'! I've got the beam turned right through the arctic circle; now I'll have to drop it for from now on we shall go through the roof of the world and down towards the other side of the Earth. I have a feeling that the Z-ray penetrating right through the Earth to the other side of the world will not produce such a convincing effect. Anyway, we'll see.'

His assumption proved to be right, for as the Z-ray moved down and began to incorporate North America and the United States, and Mexico, and so gradually swept into the daylight regions of the world and began to cross the Indian Ocean to Australia, it became perfectly obvious that the views had taken on a 'leaning backwards' appearance. Until finally when Australia itself was reached the scenes on the screen were extraordinary indeed. They depicted everything from the ground up. It was as though the transmitting end was placed deep down under the city and was looking up at the sky. To study people was absolutely impossible for they became simply a scurrying mass of feet with a background of white daylight sky behind them, whilst buildings loomed enormous at the base and narrowed away to the remotest pinpoint at the summit.

'Which proves absolutely that our beam is never stopped by a solid object,' Curtis commented in satisfaction. 'By contacting Australia it is passing right through the nickel-iron core of the Earth itself and is only stopped by the electronic vibration which constantly moves with it. I have attuned the electronic vibration to the distance away from Australia and on the screen there we behold of the result. Not a particularly good one, either,' he finished as he surveyed the huge bases of the buildings and the scurrying feet like black marks moving over a brightly lighted mirror.

'Perhaps,' Christine said, thoughtfully, 'there ought be a way of correcting that inverted appearance, possibly by sending the beam upwards somehow and catching the reflection from another point?'

'Yes, possibly,' Curtis agreed slowly,

coming over towards where she and Dick were seated; 'that is something I shall have to work out.'

'On the other hand,' Dick said, musing, 'you might perhaps use a system of prisms or something of that nature.'

Curtis wandered back to the instrument and switched it off, then he turned slowly and surveyed his sister and Dick as they both sat lost in thought.

'The modifications that will be necessary will be a small thing compared to the enormity of the discovery which we have made,' he said. 'I have to admit that all credit in the first instance goes to Chris here, even if her original idea was to use this for internal viewing of the human body, and to me of course goes the credit for having made the invention possible. To you, Dick, goes the honor of having found by sheer accident the most amazing television equipment ever devised, for if you had not tripped over that cable and swung the apparatus as you did we should still not be aware of the amazing possibilities of this invention.'

'Right enough,' Christine confirmed promptly. 'So the thing to do now is to get the modifications made and then inform the Metropolitan Television Company. After which we can sit back and watch the millions roll in.'

Curtis grinned a little. 'All very praiseworthy and all very commercial, Chris, but it doesn't happen to coincide with my own idea.'

'Why,' Dick asked, bluntly, 'what other proposition do you suggest?'

'I suggest this!' Curtis came over to them and reseated himself on his chair. 'Doesn't it occur to either of you that, having happened upon an all-seeing eye, we can look in on anybody anywhere at any moment, whether by day or by night and observe exactly what they are doing? Do you not also see that in that there stems the greatest weapon of justice ever known? We three here can literally sit in judgment upon the rest of the world, because, without anybody being aware of it, we can at any time we choose observe exactly what that person is doing. How under those circumstances can any man or woman commit a crime, pursue an immoral purpose or — cutting it short — do anything that is against the law?'

Dick and Christine nodded slowly as they looked at each other. Christine however was not looking particularly sanguine.

'It doesn't seem to me, Curt, that that will be any great financial benefit to us if we set ourselves up as sort of ubiquitous judges over anybody else. Besides I, myself, would not feel capable of filling such a position. Who are we, because we happen to possess a super instrument, that we should decide what other people ought to do? It savours of dictatorship!'

Curtis sighed. 'It's a funny thing but whenever I suggest to Sis that such and such an idea might benefit humanity she always comes back at me with the observation about dictatorship. Do you know, Dick, I get the feeling at times that my dear little sister does not altogether trust me.'

'As a matter of fact,' Christine said, bluntly, 'your dear little sister does not! And if I must be frank, the very last thing that I can imagine you doing, Curt, is setting yourself up as the guardian of public morals. Even less can I understand you doing it when there is no financial return to be gained thereby. If indeed we do use this instrument for the benefit of humanity at large, then it ought to be handed over to those whose job it is to dispense justice in the everyday way. In other words, Metropolitan Scotland Yard and let them name their figure for this invention.'

'Or if that fails,' Dick added, 'you can try the War Office and offer it as a means of defence. After all, it would be very useful to have an instrument like this at field headquarters, and know ahead of time exactly what the enemy General was trying to work out.'

Curtis shook his head slowly. 'All the money that Metropolitan Scotland Yard or the War Office could offer for this invention could not possibly come anywhere near the amount I could make out of it by handling it in my own way.'

He got to his feet suddenly waving his hands in a dramatic gesture. 'Why the possibilities are endless! It's only as time goes on and you think back on what the instrument can do that you can see the prospects ahead of us. We have right here in our hands the means of going through doors, of penetrating the deepest secrets, of looking in on the most sacrosanct regions of the world. The great mysterious lands of the Orient, the sinister dives of the criminal world, the holiest of holies! Not one of those things can escape us.'

Dick made an irritated movement. 'It's all very well getting melodramatic, Curt, but let's consider the situation a little more clearly. After all, just looking at a particular scene will not tell us much, and even if we were the witnesses of, say, a murder it wouldn't get us very far beyond having a description of the person committing the crime, which I suppose we could circulate to Metropolitan Scotland Yard. We could never use this instrument as it should be used until we also have sound with it. If we could hear as accurately as we can see then indeed we would have a weapon of terrifying power.'

'Exactly what I was thinking,' Curtis agreed. 'And it seems to me without going too deeply into the problem that the matter of sound can be dealt with. After all, vision and sound are very closely linked, and there is the gamble that after a good deal of hard concentration and probably several failures I would be able to add sound to this all-seeing eye.'

'And then what?' Christine was looking plainly uneasy. 'You get the sound added to the vision and you get the all-powerful weapon, but doesn't it occur to you that, even if that be so, you may have to spend the rest of your life waiting for that sublime coincidence whereby you happen upon an occurrence which is worthy of reporting to Metropolitan Scotland Yard, or else advertising to the world in general? You cannot possibly know when or where a murder is to be committed — since it seems to be murders that we're dealing with at the moment — nor can you possibly know the advent of an immoral circumstance, which perhaps you might be able to stop in time. It all relies upon chance. And it seems to me that it would be far simpler and far better financially if you perfected the invention and then sold it to a recognized authoritative body.'

Curtis' face was grimly resolute. 'Thank you for the valued suggestion, but I am thoroughly resolved with what I intend to do. Governments and Police Forces merely pay a fixed fee for inventions no matter how brilliant they may be, which is supposed to be perfectly satisfactory to the inventor, the inventor having the joy of realizing that he has served his country.' Curtis gave a cynical smile. 'Not for me, thank you. Even if I made several millions out of an invention like this I shouldn't consider myself repaid when in a saner moment I came to ponder how much I had lost. No, I have some very good ideas in mind for this Eye, and I mean to put them into effect.'

★ ★ ★

For nearly two weeks after that first amazing evening Curtis devoted every spare moment of his time to solving how to link sound to the electronic re-transmission of light photons. To this end he bent every vestige of his scientific skill together with his far-reaching knowledge of television. Christine and Dick continued with their own television experiments exchanging news and views with other 'Ham' operators in all parts of the world. They did not interfere with Curtis' activities in the least, nor did they ask him any questions. As far as Dick was concerned he was not particularly bothered anyway since his main interest outside the hobby of amateur television was Christine herself. Christine however, knowing her brother's scientific capabilities and also his complete lack of scruples, was far more worried than she ever admitted openly. She was reasonably sure also that Curtis would finally discover how to link sound to vision, and when he did the Eye would become the most potent scientific eavesdropper ever devised.

'I think,' Curtis said, nearly six weeks after the night of the great experiment, 'that I have accomplished the necessary modification.'

He made the announcement quite casually towards the end of an evening of television reception and transmission.

Dick turned and looked across to the opposite end of the medium-sized laboratory where Curtis was putting the finishing touches to his complicated switchboard.

'If you have got sound as well, it will be the biggest accomplishment ever! Don't you think so, Chris?'

Christine nodded, but she did not make any comment. Curtis gave a glance towards her then gave his usual wry smile.

'I do believe that dear little sister is getting worried again,' he commented, straightening up. 'You take an awful responsibility upon yourself, Chris, trying to dictate my life and deciding what I shall do. There are two very good reasons why you shouldn't. One is that I run my own life in my own way, and the other is that I am five years older than you are and therefore know a great deal more.'

Christine flushed a little, but she still did not make any comment.

'Any limitations as to how far the sound can reach?' Dick asked, strolling over to the instrument.

'Not that I can see. In fact wherever there is air the sound ought automatically to be returned along the electronic beam complete with vision, which also means that there will be complete synchronism.'

'What kind of a system have you adopted?' Christine enquired.

'The comparatively simple one of electrically transposing the air vibrations which travel along the electronic beam with the light photons, or is that too complicated?'

'I was not aware that air vibrations did travel along the electronic beam,' Christine remarked, also walking across to the instrument and studying it.

'Well of course they do! There is air within the electronic beam as much as there is outside it. A vacuum isn't created, therefore the air vibration which exists at the point of incidence of the Z-ray must be reflected back along the beam and be capable of transformation into the original vibration. Essentially, it is glorified radio linked to electronic reflection of light waves. Anyhow, to cut the scientific part short — which I am sure neither of you fully understand — take a look at this and tell me what you think of it?'

Curtis moved to the newly designed pointer system on the equipment and very carefully adjusted it. There was also another modification immediately beneath this pointer in the shape of a relief map of England. Upon the relief map were inset various numbers that corresponded with the numbers on the scale above the pointer control.

'In these past few weeks,' Curtis said, 'I have made many improvements, not the least of them being this pointer system which now gives me a range up to 8,000 miles, a range of slightly more than the diameter of the Earth. That means that I can direct the Z-ray and its accompanying electronic vibratory beam to any point on the Earth's surface that I choose. At the moment I am only including England — as you will see from the map. Later on I intend to be able to include the whole world from here to Australia.'

'Incidentally what about that leaning-back effect in the Antipodes?' Christine asked. 'Did you find a way to overcome it?'

'Unfortunately, no.' Curtis looked somewhat troubled. 'I tried every means I could think of including the reflection system which you suggested and also a device operating through prisms which I calculated would turn the scene the right way up, but I was quite unsuccessful. In any case I don't see any particular reason for going as far as Australia for our information so for the moment I shall confine myself to an area where the picture more or less remains normally upright. Now — ' Curtis snapped a switch — 'just tell me what you think of this. I am concentrating on a spot which all of us know intimately well, namely Piccadilly Circus.'

The generator hummed, the screen livened, and abruptly a night view of the hub of London appeared on the screen. Almost simultaneously the speaker that had been fitted above the screen also came to life and with it the constant roar of traffic and all the familiar noises of a great city. Curtis grinned a little as he saw the astonished looks on the faces of Dick and Christine.

'Satisfied?' he enquired, laconically.

'It's as clear as a sound track!' Christine exclaimed. 'Every single sound perfectly reproduced.'

'Sounds all right in the mass, so to speak,' Dick commented. 'But can you narrow it down so as to pick up one single conversation? That ought to be the acid test indeed.'

'No reason why not. Just listen to this . . . '

Again Curtis busied himself with the control board, changing both the view and the sound. It looked upon the screen as though a zoom lens were in operation, for suddenly from the wide angled view of Piccadilly Circus the scene began to narrow down to a man and a woman standing talking on the edge of the pavement. To begin with they had been merely two people amidst the crowd, but now as the fine focus equipment on the apparatus converged to almost its narrowest point they automatically seemed to leap upwards, retaining clarity all the time, until they were perfectly in view as head and shoulders. As this view changed the sound also changed with it, merging from the roar of the city into two voices becoming gradually more distinct until at last they were perfectly audible though there hung behind them the constant but unobtrusive roar of the traffic.

'Yes, that suits me fine,' the girl was saying, and her pretty face was lightened by a merry smile. She was young, definitely good-looking and obviously stylish. The young man beside her was smiling too, the floodlight catching the blond waves of his hair.

'All right then,' the young man said. 'We can make it the Apex Cabaret at ten o'clock tonight, and don't forget that we don't want Tommy with us, either.'

'I won't,' the girl laughed. 'Bye for now, Jimmy; it's been wonderful seeing you again — and it will be even more wonderful tonight!'

With that they shook hands and parted. Curtis reached out his hand and snapped off the equipment, his thin, sardonic face with the intelligent eyes was smiling again, cynically as usual.

'I just wonder what the outside-broadcast television boys of the old days would have made of an instrument like this,' he murmured. 'We require no transmitter from the point of transmission, and can also go through any locked door, anywhere. Now we have sound added to the device it surely is perfectly obvious that we are in a position to hold the whole world to ransom!'

'I thought,' Dick remarked, 'that your idea was to improve the morals of the community in general? That we were to sit in judgment upon our fellow men?'

'That did seem to be the original idea,' Curtis agreed, 'but since I have perfected this instrument so extraordinarily well, I do not feel inclined to use it solely to help other men and women to stay decent. What I do propose to do is make them so thoroughly uncomfortable when they do not do the right thing that they will be willing to pay me to cover up their indiscretions.'

'What,' Christine asked, deliberately, 'do you mean by that?'

'I mean,' Curtis said slowly, coming across to her and then contemplating her steadily, 'that I have evolved a 'soak the rich' policy. In other words, it is perfectly obvious that if we happen to catch somebody out in a criminal act, we could gain nothing from it if that somebody were in poor circumstances. On the other hand if we happen to alight upon somebody who is worth a good deal of money, that person will be more than willing to pay me whatever sum I might ask in order that I may keep quiet.'

'But that's blackmail,' Dick cried, astounded.

'Yes, I believe it does go under that term,' Curtis acknowledged, nodding. 'However, by whatever term it goes under I still think it is the best method to adopt. We are, of course, as my dear little sister originally foresaw, somewhat limited by the fact that we cannot choose our victim beforehand, nor have any knowledge that such and such a crime or immorality is about to be committed. We can only rely on chance. But when you come to consider the number of crimes that there are in the course of a week, even in this great city alone, we would be ill-favored indeed if we didn't happen to alight on one of them somewhere, and then proceed to make capital out of it.'

'I for one will have nothing to do with this,' Christine said flatly.

'No?' Curtis looked at her and raised his eyebrows. 'I rather think that you will, my dear. If I propose to make a great deal of money out of the indiscretions of other people, you will certainly be a fool if you walk out on the riches that can accrue from such a policy. For instance, let us suppose that Mr. Blank spends his evenings with a certain young lady who is not his wife and let us suppose on the other hand that Mr. Blank would give anything in the world to prevent his wife knowing of his indiscretion?

'Well now, when we have the facts we can not only take a cine-reel of whatever we happen upon, but we can also record it in sound, retain a copy of that film and show a duplicate film to the Mr. Blank in question. I feel perfectly sure that he will be quite willing to pay a reasonable figure for silence, and if in his rage he was successful in destroying the film which had just been shown him, it wouldn't matter in the least whilst we have a copy here. You see, if you put the goods in the window — in this case in the shape of a film in sound of the actual incident — the victim has no chance whatever to escape. Let us further assume that Mr. Blank is charged one hundred thousand pounds for absolute guaranteed silence about the incident, that will mean that between us we shall have some thirty-three-thousand pounds each, the odd thousand over going towards the expense of using the equipment, getting the film, and so forth. Quite a profitable line of business, don't you think?'

'Profitable or otherwise, it still amounts to blackmail,' Dick said, flatly, 'I don't for one moment like the idea.'

'Oh, why be so damned silly?' Curtis demanded angrily. 'If I was suggesting that we should start making money out of a lot of innocent people, or unfortunate old-age pensioners, or threatening to take the life-savings of an old couple or something like that, I could understand you getting up in arms, but in the case like this I am merely proposing to make money out of the indiscretions of people who ought to know better. And what's wrong with that?'

'It's against the law and in itself it is just as immoral as the person against whom it is directed,' Christine snapped.

'Ah, the voice of dear little sister,' Curtis exclaimed, spreading his hands. 'I thought it wouldn't be long before I was called to account. Get your head out of the clouds, Chris, and come down to earth! We have in our hands the greatest weapon of all time and it can give us untold millions, and at the same time prevent a lot of people making fools of themselves more than once. Those people who have to pay up for their indiscretions will ceaselessly wonder how they were ever discovered and even more so how a film in sound was ever taken of their actions. Believe me it will do more to level crime in this country — and in time throughout the world — than any invention ever known.'

3

The first victim

'After all,' Dick said, as he beheld Christine hesitating, 'we probably don't like the idea because it goes against our conception of what is the law. Curtis, here, may have the right idea in saying that in putting down crime and immorality — no matter by what means we do it — we are literally rendering a service to the community. And definitely there is the matter of the financial return. Thinking it over I am not quite so inclined to call it blackmail as I was at first.'

'At last a sensible observation,' Curtis said, spreading his hands, then he lowered them as he beheld Christine looking at him steadily.

'You can call it exactly what you like, Curt, and so can you Dick, but I still say it's blackmail and I don't really want any part of it. The only trouble is that since my family life and activities are so closely bound up with you two I have no choice but to tag along with you.'

'I feel sure,' Curtis remarked, 'that you will not be averse to collecting the financial returns which will accrue. Within a few years, if we play our cards correctly, we can both be worth a very considerable amount of money, and providing that we preserve the secret, which it's in all our interests to do, nobody will ever guess how our 'little tricks' are accomplished.'

For a moment there was silence, Dick hesitating and rubbing the back of his blond head slowly and somewhat perplexedly, Curtis entirely self-assured and Christine frankly doubtful. Then at last Dick stirred himself and posed a further question:

'You said we should still have to rely on chance and that you had developed a 'soak the rich' policy? Are we to understand from that that you have somebody in view whom you intend to ... er ... I will not say blackmail — whom you intend to deal with?'

'Definitely I have,' Curtis responded. 'I think, for instance, that it might be well worth our while to follow the private activities of one Samuel T. Wernham.'

Christine and Dick nodded slowly. Samuel T. Wernham was known well enough to them, as indeed he must have been to the great mass of the newspaper-reading public. The more scandal-mongering rags had never openly published his private life, but there had nevertheless been countless hints in the gossip columns that all was not as it should be in the life of this famous and extremely wealthy industrialist. To the eyes of the world he was a sedate married man, with two grown-up daughters, but the eternal army of muckrakers had long since discovered that he did many questionable things on the side. Possibly an ubiquitous Eye that could follow him wherever he went would bring to light some astounding, not to say sordid, facts.

'I think,' Curtis continued, after a momentary pause, 'that Samuel T. is a most likely prospect. In the first place he has a doubtful life as the newspapers have hinted, and in the second place he is worth several millions. For him our price could be high. Further, we know exactly where he lives, which makes the matter of pinpointing the apparatus not at all difficult; therefore my suggestion is that commencing tomorrow evening we pick up Samuel T. Wernham from the moment he goes home — or rather leaves his office in the city — and then proceed to watch exactly what he does. And, of course, also listen to what he has to say. It's more than possible that it should prove very interesting.'

'Why tomorrow?' Dick enquired. 'What's wrong with tonight?'

'Nothing, except the fact that it is now nearly nine o'clock and I should imagine that by now Samuel T. will have embarked on whatever evening escapade he had in mind. No, far better to do it tomorrow and start off round about two-thirty in the afternoon, tuning the beam on to the Wernham Financial Trust Building where his headquarters are, and keep a constant watch until he leaves his business premises. After that we keep him in the beam all the time. Half past two will be a difficult hour for me but I think that I shall be able to manage it for once — in fact I'll take damned good care I do. Once we get this organization of ours comfortably working we shall have no need to be at the behest of other people and work ourselves to death just so that our employers can make more money. This is the supreme method by which we can become independent. I hope you're listening, darling sister.'

'Yes, I'm listening,' Christine acknowledged coolly. 'Come to think of it, Curt, your idea is a good one in some ways but a distinctly unscrupulous one in others. However, as I said, I'll tag along with you. I'll also see if I can get time off tomorrow afternoon so that I can be with you and watch what happens. How about you Dick?'

Dick rubbed his chin. 'Yes . . . Maybe I can manage something. I'll do my best anyhow.'

'All of this,' Curtis said, 'calls for a drink. I think the sooner we retire into the house and toast the Eye, the better.'

So it was that the most incredible scientific invention to date began its sinister and completely secret career . . .

Entirely unaware that he had been singled out as the first victim of the Eye, Samuel T. Wernham left the Wernham Financial Trust Building at 3.15 the following afternoon and departed majestically down the steps of the mighty edifice to his limousine parked outside. He had no possible means of knowing that at this time three young scientists were grouped together in a small laboratory in the north of London and were watching his every move intently through the Eye screen. At the same time the sounds of the main street were passing through the speaker but presently Samuel T. Wernam's own voice was distinctly heard as he spoke to his own chauffeur.

'You have your instructions, Barnes. You know exactly what to do?'

'Yes, sir. Drive you home and then ring you up at precisely five-thirty with an urgent business call.'

The financier grinned. 'It's surprising

how many urgent business calls I've had in the last two months, Barnes. However, as you are a sensible man I know that you will keep it entirely to yourself, especially considering the financial reimbursement which is due to you for your allegiance.'

'Yes, sir,' Barnes agreed woodenly. 'I am only too delighted to be of service, sir.'

Upon which the financier got into his car and Barnes dutifully closed the door upon him. In a moment or two the great car was on its way but it could not evade the relentless Eye which followed it as it pursued its course through the dense city traffic, only coming to a halt nearly half an hour later at a tremendous modern mansion just clear of the main huddle of the suburban area.

Back in the laboratory Dick gave a broad smile as the beam followed the financier like a tracking camera into the hall of his enormous residence.

'Begins to look to me, Curt, as though you had a good idea here,' he commented, glancing across at him as he fixedly watched the screen and listened to the loudspeaker. 'That urgent business call may be the very thing that we're waiting for to pin Samuel T. down to something that he ought not to be doing!'

'That's what I'm hoping for,' Curtis responded. He went across to the recording cine camera and checked it over to be sure that at an instant's notice it could be switched on so that the scenes and sounds emanating from the receiver could be photographed on negative film. From this negative any number of positive copies could be made and if indeed he did commit an indiscretion Samuel T. Wernham would find himself utterly incapable of any defense.

'I wish,' Christine sighed, as she saw the two men inspecting the cine camera, 'that I could decide what it is this business which strikes me as being so odious. I know perfectly well that we're following the movements of a man who leads a double life, but I also have the horribly slimy feeling that I'm looking on something that I shouldn't be. I feel just about as comfortable as if I were having a bath in the middle of Leicester Square.'

Curt glanced at her briefly. 'If you'd stop making idiotic similes, Chris, and concentrate on the fact that money we shall accrue is from a man who is leading an immoral life and is worth several millions, maybe you'd get things in better focus. There's nothing slimy or unscrupulous about what we are doing, for the simple reason that if the people we watch are not doing anything wrong, there is no reason why they should fear being watched and even less reason why we should refrain from watching them. The whole thing's perfectly logical when you come to think it out.'

'To your kind of mind maybe,' Christine responded, 'or perhaps that's just a masculine outlook which I am incapable of understanding. However, let us see what Samuel T. is going to do next.'

As it happened Samuel T. did not do anything very extraordinary — in fact he seemed the mildest and most pleasant of husbands during the next hour that followed. He treated his wife exactly as he should then he retired to his study and spent quite a while dealing with obvious matters, finally closing down on his correspondence at five o'clock. Since it was plain that he was not supposed to anticipate the telephone call which was due at five thirty he made no attempt to change from the lounge suit in which he had done his day's business; instead he moved from the library to the lounge and there settled himself to read the early edition of the evening paper until, presumably, dinner should be served. Opposite him sat his wife, a thin-nosed woman with graying hair, who had upon her once lovely countenance an expression of resigned despair. It was more than clear from the intimate close-ups which Curtis succeeded in obtaining that Mrs. Wernham was not finding her position as the wife of a famous industrialist a particularly comfortable one.

At exactly five-thirty a telephone call came through as arranged. After he had taken it in the library Samuel T. returned into the lounge with an expression of regret on his big, dogged face.

'So sorry my dear . . . ' He spread his

71

hands and looked at his wife contritely, 'that was Beamish on the telephone. I'm afraid I shall have to spend the evening with him trying to sort out that deal concerning Copper Consolidated. You will not mind too much?'

'I have little choice, Samuel,' his wife replied shrugging.

For a moment the big man hesitated, looking at his wife intently, as though trying to divine whether she guessed his real intentions. Then he gave his big, disarming grin.

'I am afraid, my dear, that my constant departures in the evening are just one of the many penalties of your being married to a most important man.'

He stooped and kissed her forehead perfunctorily then turned and left the lounge. Just for a moment Curtis turned the Z-ray to where Mrs. Wernham sat in her chair, apparently reading, and the fine focus close-up that he obtained showed the undoubted bitterness in that lady's eyes.

Then the scene quickly switched and swept up the stairs on the track once more of Samuel T. himself. After some searching with the controls he was picked up in one of the many bathrooms of the great residence, busily shaving himself and smiling genially at his reflection in the mirror.

'Little doubt what that old lad's up to,' Dick commented refreshingly, as hands in pockets he still stood watching the screen. 'It will be even more interesting to see what his business appointment really is. I can't imagine that it's genuine, otherwise he wouldn't look so happy about it. I never saw an industrialist grinning to himself the way he's doing when he has a business deal ahead of him. Usually they look like a bulldog with the stomach-ache.'

'If you're going to follow him the whole time, and if he's going to retire to his room and change,' Christine remarked, looking rather embarrassed, 'I think I'd better go and prepare some refreshment for us. I've stood about as much as I can already of looking into another person's home without permission. And I'm certainly not going to invade privacy in every possible way.'

With that she got to her feet, gave Curtis a cold and meaning glance, then left the laboratory and closed the door sharply.

'There are times,' Curtis remarked, his eyes absently on the screen as he watched Samuel T. shaving, 'when I feel almost inclined to hit my dear little sister. I just can't understand where she gets her independent attitude from, you know. Mother and father, when they were alive — God bless 'em! — were both surprisingly matter-of-fact people who had no particular scruples so long as they could make a fairly comfortable living. That's Christine's trouble; she's always wandering round with that chip on her shoulder.'

'Chip or no chip,' Dick said, wagging his head, 'she suits me fine. And she'll suit me even better when we're married.'

'I take it from that,' Curtis remarked dryly, 'that the prospect of your having me as a brother-in-law does not terrify you.'

'Terrify me?' Dick laughed outright.

'Why on earth should it? I've no bone to pick with you Curt; I think you're one of the cleverest scientific engineers I have ever known — as the Eye here shows. I'm sure there's nothing to really worry about with regard to Christine; it's just that being a girl, and a quiet, well-brought up one at that, she doesn't get the hang of what we're doing. After all, it isn't particularly surprising; it is an unorthodox way of making a living after all.'

'But a dashed good one,' declared Curtis, clenching his fists. 'A very good one!'

He did not say anything more for the moment, for, his shaving completed, Samuel T. strode along the long hotel-like corridor of his home and presently entered in his immense bedroom. Here his valet moved with soundless efficiency, and in the course of perhaps another ten minutes Samuel T. Wernham had been transformed from his lounge suit into immaculate evening dress, his graying hair brushed tightly to his very round head.

'A dash of eau-de-cologne and he'll be all set,' Dick remarked, with a somewhat sour glance. 'I never saw such a lot of palaver for a man to go through. It must be a woman he's going to meet. Curt; he'd never go to all this trouble, just to meet a business associate!'

'We'll see in time,' Curtis replied, and he glanced across to the laboratory door as Christine came in again, bearing with her a tray upon which were piled up sandwiches and three steaming cups of coffee.

'Well,' she asked, without glancing at the screen, 'has Samuel T. made himself decent?'

'I doubt if Samuel T. will ever do that,' Curtis replied, grinning. 'If you mean is he reasonably dressed, yes. You can look at the screen without being shocked,' he added dryly.

Christine glanced, shrugged, then looked away again. It was obvious that her interest in this scientific eavesdropping was becoming less and less acute as time passed.

'Sandwiches?' she asked briefly, nodding towards them and seating herself at the small table.

The two men nodded, but whilst Dick

came over to the table to join her, Curtis remained by the apparatus, since it was necessary he should keep his hand on the Z-ray control if he was to continue to follow the activities of Samuel T. Wernham.

Back in his home Samuel T. Wernham was sublimely confident of himself and on looking in the mirror he very much admired the reflection that was given back to him. The dressing stage over he wasted no more time and following a brief farewell with his wife he took his departure from the house and settled once more in the limousine with the inscrutable Barnes at the wheel.

Relentlessly the Eye followed him from the residence, down the main streets and into the city traffic, and still held him pin-pointed as eventually the superb car drew up outside Marcati's Hotel in the center of the city. This was quite one of the most exclusive spots and frequented only by the high and mighty. Every sound, every gesture, every word of the great industrialist was recorded as he presently arrived at the second-floor of the hotel and went along to the door numbered 3A. Evidently everything was pre-arranged for he withdrew a key from his pocket and entered the room, the penetrating beam passing clean through the wall and following him as he began to move about the superbly furnished lounge of this sumptuous suite.

It was now six-thirty and for the next hour Samuel T. kept himself busy on the telephone, ordering flowers, explaining to the waiter how they should be arranged when they were brought; then taking his time ordering the hotel's most exclusive dinner.

'And remember,' Samuel T. finished as the waiter was about to take his departure. 'I am not on any account to be disturbed. The moment Miss Grayson arrives be good enough to show her to this room and serve the dinner within ten minutes of her arrival. Do you understand?'

'Perfectly, Mr. Wernham,' the waiter agreed calmly.

'Good,' the financier grinned broadly. 'Here you are . . . invest that in munitions shares and in a few years you'll be a wealthy man like me.'

The waiter gave an enigmatic smile. 'There are possibilities, sir, in the hotel business,' he replied ambiguously, and with that he took his departure.

'I think,' Curtis remarked, as he, Christine, and Dick sat watching the screen, the business of the sandwiches and coffee long since dealt with, 'that we are now nearing the point where one of us must stand near the cine camera. How about you, Chris, will you take that over?'

'I prefer not to,' she answered briefly.

Curtis gave her an angry look. 'If you're not prepared to take any part in the proceedings, Chris, you cannot possibly expect any financial return. Either do your share of the hard work or else . . . '

'Or else — what?'

'I just don't know,' Curtis muttered. 'I can't tell you to leave when you live in the same house as I do, but on the other hand I think the least you can do is be reasonable.'

'Nothing to worry about anyway,' Dick

remarked. 'I can take over the cine camera. Just press the remote control and that's that.'

'A great deal more than that,' Curtis told him. 'I want you to watch over the sound-recording system to make sure that we get it all down. You'll have to keep your eye on that volume oscillator there, to make sure that the voices are properly recorded. It's an absolutely essential point that we get the sound correct. It takes three of us to handle this business,' he went on, looking at his sister and then at Dick grimly. 'One to control the Z-ray apparatus — which is me — and the other to control the camera and make sure that it is constantly set on the screen, and another to watch the sound record-ing, so are you going to be a part, Chris, or not?'

She sighed and got to her feet. 'Oh, very well, if that's the way you want it.' She went over to the camera and inspected it, then Curtis indicated the control knob set at the camera's side.

'All you have to do is turn that,' he explained. 'The moment you do so the camera will come into action, being driven by that electric generator there. It will keep on running as long as there is film in it, and since there is a good thousand feet of film in those specially made cassettes, we should have enough for about twenty minutes continuous action. When that reel runs off you'll press that right hand knob there which will bring a subsidiary reel into action so that the filming can be non-stop. Is that plain enough or do you want it in writing?'

'There are many things I would like in writing,' Christine commented, shrugging, 'but this doesn't happen to be one of them.'

Further conversation ceased abruptly as things began to happen on the screen. They began with the buzz of the doorbell of the suite and Samuel T. Wernham immediately crossed to the door and opened it. Upon the threshold stood a young and very pretty woman dressed in the height of fashion. She smiled warmly as Samuel T. looked upon her, then he gently ushered her into the room and closed the door behind her.

'Earlier than I had expected, Effie,' he exclaimed, embracing her. 'Not that that matters! All the better!'

'Right,' Curtis said briefly, glancing at his sister. 'Get that camera going, quick. Dick, get across to that sound recording and see that everything's in order.'

By the time this had been done Samuel T. had relieved Effie Grayson of her costly fur coat and had motioned to the settee.

'This,' Curtis commented, smiling tautly, 'is one of the nicest things I have ever seen. I'm sure Samuel T. will be only too pleased to delve into his pockets very deeply, for a worthy cause, when he gets the film of this lot.'

Christine returned her gaze to the screen. Curtis stood looking at her for a moment, then he shrugged to himself and also turned to watch the intimate association which was depicted by the Z-ray from London's costliest hotel.

The remainder of the details, which lasted nearly an hour and a half and used up cassette after cassette of film in the camera was something that Christine found most disturbing to watch. Even Dick did not spend all his time watching the screen. Curtis, however, remained constantly in position, his hands closed on the control switch moving in to close-ups and long distance shots, making sure that the camera recorded every one of them. Nor did he give the signal to stop until Samuel T and Effie Grayson had left the suite together and were on their way to the elevator.

'I think,' Curtis remarked, switching off the Z-ray, 'that we have here everything that we could need. The point to weigh up now is — from what we have photographed, in sound, how much we can reasonably expect from Samuel T. Wernham in return for the original negative?'

'This gets intolerable!' Christine exclaimed angrily, striding across to the table and flinging herself into the chair. 'Not content with turning this ubiquitous Eye into the privacy of that suite you now start to work out in cold bargaining terms just how much that tycoon's immorality is worth to us! I just won't have anything to do with it, Curt. Absolutely nothing!'

'Just as you like, my dear.' Curtis shrugged, also coming to the table and sitting down thoughtfully. 'I should have thought myself that thirty thousand pounds each — plus say, five thousand for expenses — for this night's work ought to be considered a reasonable figure and one that ought to tempt you to forget your very high elevation of ethics. If on the other hand you do not wish to have anything to do with the idea, then Dick and I can split the money two ways with the odd thousand for expenses. It's entirely up to you but I warn you that if you leave us you will also automatically leave this house and go and live wherever you choose. We would hardly be content to stay under the same roof. Don't forget that I am your brother, the house, by the will of father is my own, and I can order you out of it if I wish to. If you do go and speak to anybody outside of this Z-ray and what it can do it will be most — uncomfortable for you, my dear.'

'What kind of a threat do you call that?' Dick asked angrily. 'You seem to forget that Christine and I are engaged. I've a great deal to do with her protection as well. Remember that!'

Curtis looked at him coldly. 'I always had the impression, Dick, that you're a sensible fellow. Not particularly brilliant perhaps, but willing and genial enough. Are you also prepared to throw up all the financial returns you can get all because of a silly young girl's whim?'

'I'm not a silly young girl, nor is it a whim,' Christine retorted. 'I grew out of the teenage stage long ago. It's just that I'm convinced deep down that this is the rottenest, filthiest way of making a living that there can be! Why, it's worse than the ordinary blackmailer when you come to weigh it up. He has nothing more than the facts to go upon, while this simply goes right through closed doors and all barriers and sneaks up in the dark. No one stands a chance against it. There are moments when I feel I would like to wreck the whole apparatus!'

'Even if you did do that it could always be built again.' Curtis looked at her with venom in his dark eyes. Then suddenly his hard expression relaxed a little. 'For heaven's sake, Chris, be sensible,' he pleaded. 'We've been through it over and over again what we're driving at and, if it comes to that, I suppose it is a somewhat filthy business. There used to be a saying in the old days that where the dirt is, the money is. I think this is one of the best examples of it!'

Christine was silent for a long moment, deliberating. Then at last she sighed.

'All right, you win.' She spread her hands. 'It doesn't suit me to leave this house and since I'm not absolutely crawling with money I may as well have a bit more if there's any chance of getting it. How much did you say you were going to rook Samuel T. for? Ninety-five thousand?'

'That's it,' Curtis agreed. 'That gives us thirty thousand pounds apiece, with five thousand for expenses. If that's agreed amongst us I'll go and see him tomorrow and find out exactly what I can do.'

'You'll go and see him?' Dick repeated, staring. 'Isn't that one hell of a risk to take?'

'Why should it be? He doesn't know me from Adam.'

'Not to begin with, certainly,' Dick agreed, 'but once you start making a demand of him for that kind of money I should think he's the kind of man who'd make it his business to know all about you, what you do, how you've found out what you have, and all the rest of it.'

'You think so?' Curtis gave a sardonic smile. 'Unless I'm very much mistaken, that bird will be only too glad to pay up, take the negative of the film and destroy it. He'll be so baffled, so scared, that his innermost life has been so relentlessly photographed and recorded that he won't dare to make investigations for fear of what I might be able to do. I'm absolutely confident of getting away with it even if you are not.'

'I'm not either; that makes two of us,' Christine remarked. 'And there's another point which I don't like about this. If Samuel T. does go the whole hog and discovers all about you, it will inevitably drag in Dick and me as well. I don't like the contemplation of that prospect one little bit.'

'Possibly not — but the fact remains

that you're both in it as much as I am. Whatever the risks I take you take also. Now let's have no more of this arguing back and forth. We're agreed that I shall dun him for ninety-five thousand and whatever risks there are attached to it, I'll take as much as you do. After all I'm getting the hardest part of the job in going to interview him. I don't suppose it will be a cordial interview by any means.'

'What time do you propose to see him tomorrow?' Dick enquired.

'Oh, round about ten-thirty, when he gets to his office . . . Ah, I see what you're thinking, Dick. About my job? Matter of fact I'm not continuing with that job any more. Tonight brought an end to my working for other people. From here on I work for myself and within a year, if we can pick up a few more Samuel T. Wernhams, we shall be absolutely rolling in it.'

'Suits me,' Dick grinned, as easily led as ever, and genial all the time.

It was inevitable under these conditions that Christine, despite her independent nature and her inner feeling of revulsion at the scientific eavesdropping in which her brother was engaged, should feel herself being drawn irresistibly into Curtis' orbit. He had a definitely convincing way with him and the dream of financial wealth that he held out was something that a girl in Christine's position could not afford to entirely ignore. The wrongness of the whole thing lay not in Christine's acceptance of his methods, but in his inscrutable domination over her and his insistence that she should be carried along with him in his career of super-scientific blackmail. For that, plainly and simply, was what it was. He had turned the undoubted vast benefits of a mighty discovery to the most sordid uses, and for nothing more than financial gain and personal aggrandizement.

As to the consequences, he could not see any. Nobody but himself, his sister, and Dick knew about the invention and he was implacably determined that nobody else ever should.

'Concerning this matter of jobs,' Christine said after a moment or two, 'do you think that I would be wise in leaving mine? If we're going to make the scores of thousands that you seem to think there doesn't seem to be much point in my carrying on my everyday employment. Heaven knows I'll be glad enough to leave. I never liked the job anyway!'

Curtis rubbed his hands in delight. 'That is the first sign I have had so far that my dear little sister is willing to tag along with me,' he exclaimed. 'By all means leave your job — you can be quite sure I shall not let you down. The same goes for you, Dick, if you feel confident enough of what we have in our hands to let your normal employment go hang. Believe me, once we get really started we shall need to keep on this job more or less constantly, keeping alert for any signs of anything unusual worth following up in order to make a cash return.'

'From here on,' Dick said calmly, 'my normal job just does not exist! I'll send in my notice and forego whatever salary might be due to me so that I can devote my time entirely to our interesting little business.'

'That settles it then,' Curtis decided. 'Once I've dealt with Samuel T. Wernham we'll work out a kind of system of shifts by which one of us is always on the watch for something worthwhile to follow up. We're at the beginning of one of the greatest things ever, and once Christine has entirely outgrown her somewhat kindergarten viewpoint we'll definitely go places in a big way! That being decided I think the best thing I can do now is work out my plan of attack for tomorrow — '

'There's just one thing,' Dick said. 'Is there any reason why Chris and I cannot look in on your interview with Samuel T.? It would be extremely interesting to us just to see how the situation goes.'

Curtis shrugged. 'You could do, with pleasure, if you knew how to control the instrument. As it happens I'm the only one who knows that and I certainly haven't the time to teach you all the intricacies between now and tomorrow. No, I should forget that part of the business if I were you.'

Christine gave a quick glance. 'You will of course find the time somewhere to teach us how the thing works?'

'Obviously,' Curtis replied. 'How otherwise do you expect to be able to take your turns in controlling the instrument when you don't even know how to operate it? In the next few weeks I'll show you all about it until you become as efficient in its operation as I am.'

'What about taking out a patent for this thing?' Dick asked, thoughtfully. 'It's of immense value and you ought to protect it for all our sakes.'

'I'm aware of it, but there are various reasons against taking out a patent. For one thing I am never likely to have any competition since this discovery was made entirely by accident — and for another thing, although the Patent Offices are reputed to be beyond reproach in the matter of keeping one's confidences, I still cannot feel safe in trusting my diagrams, sketches and plans to anybody else outside us three. No, I'm not taking out any patent. I'm relying solely on the fact that this invention is a secret and that it will remain so. From that there comes the logical inference that if anybody does produce an invention almost exactly like this one and having the same powers, our particular little game will be scotched. It's only because we're entirely exclusive and absolutely secret we'll get away with it.'

On that Curtis turned to the laboratory door, motioned with his head. 'Shall we go in and get some more refreshment? Then I can start working out what I am going to say to Samuel T. on the morrow.'

4

The price of silence

It was just after ten-thirty the following morning when Curtis entered the wide granite and chromium entrance hall of the enormous Wernham Financial Trust Building. He found his path immediately blocked by a gigantic commissionaire, magnificent in bottle-green uniform and considerable amounts of gold braid.

'Your pleasure, sir?' the commissionaire enquired, deferentially.

Curtis gave his disarming smile. 'I would like a word with Mr. Wernham personally. My name is Henry Brixton.'

'You have an appointment, sir?'

'No, but I am quite sure that Mr. Wernham will see me. It is an extremely personal matter and one of great urgency. So urgent indeed,' Curtis continued, 'that I spent nearly half an hour outside this building waiting to observe Mr.

Wernham's arrival. That will obviate the necessity of telling me that he has not yet arrived or that he is out.'

The commissionaire looked Curtis up and down thoughtfully. Certainly he beheld nothing about him to which he could take objection. He was well dressed and smoothly shaven and as usual emanating that air of supreme self-confidence.

'I will enquire, sir, if Mr. Wernham is at liberty,' the commissionaire said, briefly, and turned away to the hall telephone. He was occupied with it for a few moments then came back to where Curtis was standing.

'As it happens, sir, you are lucky. Mr. Wernham is not engaged at the moment.'

'I cannot see that there is any element of luck about it when the matter is one of importance,' Curtis retorted. 'Perhaps you'll be good enough to show me the way to his office?'

The commissionaire eyed him and then nodded. Leading the way up the enormous entrance hall to the elevator, within five more minutes — since the industrialist's private office was right at the top of the great building — Curtis was being shown into the big man's presence.

He looked exactly as he had appeared on the televisor screen — round-headed, dogged-jaws, with vulgar, ostentatious rings upon his podgy fingers.

'Glad to know you, Mr. Brixton.' Samuel T. rose to his feet and came round the desk, shaking hands briskly. 'Have a seat. Cigar? Cigarette? Drink?'

'Thank you, no.' Curtis repeated calmly, settling himself and loosening his overcoat. 'I appreciate the hospitality, Mr. Wernham, but I have the feeling that by the time our conversation is ended you will perhaps not feel quite so inclined to be cordial.'

'Oh.' Wernham's brows came down abruptly. 'And why not?'

'The matter upon which I am here, Mr. Wernham, is one of extreme delicacy,' Curtis sat back in his chair, apparently completely at his ease, though he was thinking swiftly to make sure that he didn't make a single false move. He was right in the lion's den now and one mistake would put him at the industrialist's mercy.

Samuel T. returned to his chair behind the desk, snipped the end from his cigar and lighted it. Then he waited, his brooding eyes on Curtis' thin, sardonic face.

'I believe,' Curtis said, after a moment or two's reflection, 'that you are well acquainted with a young lady by the name of Miss Effie Grayson?'

The industrialist gave the slightest of starts. 'Even if I should be I cannot see that it is any concern of yours, Mr. Brixton.'

'Normally it would not be.' Curtis gave his hard smile. 'Indeed, as far as personalities are concerned you and Miss Grayson could not interest me less. It is the fact that you are both so closely connected and that you spent last evening having a little tête-à-tête together which brings me here this morning. I have in this briefcase of mine something which I would like you to see and which I am quite convinced you would not like anybody else to see.'

'What the hell are you talking about?' the financier demanded bluntly.

'Just this.' Curtis unfastened the briefcase he was carrying and from it extracted a roll of film. It was of considerable size — indeed an eighteen-hundred-foot spool. The industrialist gazed at it in blank amazement and then his mouth set tightly round his cigar.

'I have heard many strange ways to start an interview,' he said bluntly, 'but this is quite the most unique. As a salesman, my young friend, you are definitely excellent, but it so happens that I am not the least interested in a film of your products or anything else. You would oblige me by — '

'Just a minute,' Curtis interrupted. 'I am not trying to sell any product, at least not in the commercial sense. What I am trying to sell — indeed what I am quite convinced of selling — is this film to you, and indeed the original negative. You see, you and Miss Grayson happen to be the star players in it. Not only in action but also in sound. I am sure that if you can spare the time to see the film through here and now you will be extremely interested.'

Samuel T. shifted uncomfortably in his chair and then he held out a podgy hand.

'May I just see the beginning of that film?'

'No,' Curtis replied, and put the film down flat on the desk with the palm of his hand upon it. 'Just glancing at it in the ordinary way wouldn't be the slightest use. You have to see it through a sound projector and then judge for yourself. I assure you it would be very much to your advantage to do as I suggest.'

Samuel T. gave a sigh. 'Very well. But I warn you, Mr. Brixton, that if you're just wasting my time you'll certainly hear plenty about it afterwards. All right. I have a private projection theatre here for the exhibition of films concerning my business products so we may as well go there. If you'll come this way.' He got to his feet, strode to the door, and held it open, then as he passed out into the corridor, the film reel in his hand, Curtis said:

'I think it would be advisable if I ran this film through myself. That is to say I would not consider it prudent for your usual projectionist to see what is on the film.'

Samuel T. gave a grin. 'All right, carry on; I'm quite interested . . . ' He paused, his eyes hardening. 'But just a minute! Did I understand you to say that Miss Grayson and myself are the star players in this film?'

'That is exactly what I said; that is why I think it advisable that nobody else sees the picture except you and me.'

Samuel T. shrugged and said no more. He led the way down the broad corridor and eventually turned in through a doorway marked 'Projection Booth No. 1'. Switching on the lights he nodded to the steel doors, which opened into the projection room. 'You'll find everything in there, Mr. Brixton. I'll take a seat out here and after this masterpiece — whatever it may be — has been run through, we'll talk again. Is that it?'

'Suits me,' Curtis agreed calmly. 'The only other thing I would suggest is that you lock the door in case somebody should suddenly come in upon us.'

The financier turned in amazement as he was about to sit down. 'What kind of a film have you got here?' he demanded.

'Nothing more or less than a complete sound film of your tête-à-tête last night with Miss Grayson.'

The financier hesitated, scowled, then he broke into sudden uproarious laughter. 'Well, I've heard a few things,' he gasped at last, 'but this definitely caps the lot! I admit that Miss Grayson and I spent last evening together, but that you could ever have photographed it, and in sound at that, is utterly beyond all possibility!'

'I shall be interested to see if you still think the same thing in a moment or two,' Curtis remarked.

With that he turned into the projection booth and began busying himself with loading the film through the projector. Through the porthole he could see Samuel T. scratching the back of his head and finally his fleshy shoulders rose and fell in a shrug and he seated himself to await the picture.

Nor was it very long in coming. Curtis dimmed the lights and there before him Samuel T. Wernham beheld an exact repetition of everything he had done the previous evening, and the more he saw the more he writhed and muttered under his breath in growing fury. Twice he jumped up as though to have the film stopped and then he hesitated and sat down again. So, finally, it ran its course and the lights returned. Curtis calmly took the reel from the bottom spool box of the machine and wandered back into the main auditorium of the booth.

'I think,' Curtis remarked, 'that that film made things far clearer than any talking on my part would ever do.'

'You impudent upstart!' Samuel T. Wernham breathed dangerously, struggling to his feet. 'Where the hell did you get a film like that? Where did you take it? I suppose one of those infernal hotel employees managed to smuggle it in somehow. Maybe you photographed it through the mirror over the mantelpiece.'

'An ingenious thought,' Curtis commented, 'but I hardly see how I could have done that.'

'I am referring to black glass,' Samuel T. retorted. 'The kind of thing that looks like a mirror on the front yet if you're behind it you can look right through it. Many a secret filming session has been accomplished in that way. The microphone could easily be put somewhere to pick up the sound to make the recording.'

Curtis smiled infuriatingly. 'I can assure you, Mr. Wernham, that I was nowhere near the hotel.'

'Then somebody must have been, otherwise that film couldn't have been made.'

'It seems to me that the whys and wherefores of the film do not matter in the least,' Curtis said, seating himself, at which the industrialist slowly did likewise. 'What concerns us is the subject matter of the picture. I have been thinking it over carefully and I'm sure that a man in your position would not like a film like this released for public exhibition.'

'You dare show that film anywhere and

I'll have you clapped in jail before you know where you are!'

'Oh come now, Mr. Wernham ... ' Curtis made an indolent movement. 'You are a business man and you must appreciate that to report my activities to the police you would be compelled to let that film be seen and I imagine that is the last thing you would want. Now you see why I insisted on privacy. I have a proposition to make and it is this: I am prepared to give you this film and the negative film from which it was taken for the sum of ninety-five thousand pounds.'

'You can go to hell!' Samuel T. replied briefly. 'Get off my premises if you know what's good for you, and if you make one move regarding this film I'll risk all the consequences and have the police down on you before you know it.'

Curtis did not move. He withdrew a cigarette from the case in his overcoat pocket, lighted it, then sat back and considered. Beside him the industrialist shifted irritably, but he too did not rise. Then finally he muttered something under his breath and spoke out loud.

'Why the unusual sum of ninety-five thousand?' he enquired. 'I take it the odd five thousand pounds is for the expense you've been to in getting this blasted recording?'

'Nothing of the kind. It just happens to suit my purpose that it be ninety-five thousand, that's all. It's up to you Mr. Wernham. It would be a simple matter for me to publicize this film, and I remain reasonably convinced that you cannot afford to take that risk. You can afford ninety-five thousand pounds. It will be a mere button off a shirt to a man like you. I'm sure it's well worth it in order to preserve your — er — reputation.'

'For which sum I get this copy and the negative from which it was taken?'

'That's right.'

'And how am I to know that you're telling the truth? How am I to know that you have not other copies somewhere which you will produce when the mood so seizes you — or else you'll try and blackmail me further?'

'The deal starts and ends here,' Curtis replied flatly. 'I cannot give you any more than my word on that but you can rest assured that once I have received my money I shall no longer be interested. I should also add that I do not wish the ninety-five thousand pounds in the nature of a cheque. I require it in five pound notes.'

'Which is adding insult to injury,' the financier growled. 'Where do you suppose I can find ninety-five thousand in five pound notes? Why, the bank would immediately start enquiries into a thing like that.'

'A man like you can tell a bank when to open and shut,' Curtis retorted. 'Get ninety-five thousand in five pound notes and I'll remain in this building until you do so. There's every facility for me doing that since it's provided with cafeterias, lounges, and everything else that's necessary. I'm warning you, Mr. Wernham, you're in a tight spot, and I do not intend to leave here until I have satisfaction.'

Samuel T. slowly began to relax. His cigar, which by now had smoldered to the stump he removed from his mouth, jammed it in the ashtray in front of him and snipped the end from another of the weeds. His first anger had subsided now; instead he was beginning to look interested.

'All other things apart, Mr. Brixton and I assume your name is as phony as everything else about you — how did you get a cinematic record like that? I know I'm the main subject in it, and that Effie Grayson also features with startling prominence, but I really am more interested in the mechanics of the whole thing. Was it done by a process of X-rays or what? I'm absolutely sure that there was nothing in that hotel suite because I have long since felt that some kind of outrage like this would be attempted, and therefore have always examined the premises where I have indulged, shall we say — in my little feminine conferences.' He laughed unconvincingly and then continued, 'I would willingly pay you ten million for the answer to my question. And of course the formula and specifications of — '

'How it was done is no concern of yours,' Curtis interrupted. 'You have my price for silence — the rest is up to you. I have in my possession, Mr. Wernham, an invention of terrifying possibilities and being as much a businessman as yourself I intend to make the very utmost out of it. Suppose we meet again in your office in one hour, by which time I shall hope that you will have found it possible to provide the ninety-five thousand pounds in notes that I have asked for.'

'You are a businessman: I admit that,' Wernham said slowly, 'but you're also a damned fool, my young friend. You should know that a man in my position has dozens of ways of enforcing his will and you surely don't suppose for one moment that I'm going to let you get away with a stunt like this, do you? If I did not feel absolutely confident of myself I would not pay.'

'The effort is to make you pay for your indiscretion, Mr. Wernham. You can send your strong-arm men after me. You can use all the spies you possess to try and find out all they can about me, but if you do I will also expose about you so many things that you will find it necessary to call off your private war against me. I have weighed up every contingency and I am probably the only man living who can make the great Samuel T. Wernham dance to my tune. I am well aware that your indiscretions with Miss Grayson are not the only ones; there are certain matters about the stock market which if brought to light would — '

'All right.' Samuel T. growled, struggling to his feet. 'I shall have to call this a business deal and let it go at that. Return to my office in an hour as you suggested and I'll see what I can do.'

'Don't just see what you can do, Mr. Wernham; do it. Because if you haven't got what I require within an hour I shall leave this building and the evening papers will be full of a most interesting disclosure concerning one of the foremost industrialists of our time.'

*　*　*

It was towards two o'clock that afternoon when Curtis returned to his laboratory to find Dick and Christine anxiously awaiting him. The singular point was that Curtis was no longer attired in the clothes in which he had visited Samuel T. Wernham; instead he was wearing a shabby-looking tweed suit over which was carelessly flung a cheap mackintosh. At his throat was bunched a scarf, and a trilby hat was pulled well down over his eyes. He was traveling light, having no film reel or briefcase with him, indeed no packages of any kind.

'Well?' Dick asked anxiously, hurrying forward. 'So what happened? Did you see him? Did you get what you intended?'

'Naturally, otherwise I would not have gone. Curtis threw down his battered hat and tugged the scarf from his neck.

'You actually mean that you talked Samuel T. Wernham into parting with ninety-five thousand pounds?' Christine asked in amazement.

'I did, and I've spent the rest of the time since then dodging his trained army of snoopers and private detectives.'

'Then where's the money?' Dick asked, in dismay. 'I'm pretty sure that you couldn't carry the ninety-five thousand in your pocket. You said something about going to get it in five pound notes, didn't you?'

'I said that, yes, and I did. Let me tell you what happened. Samuel T. got the ninety-five thousand in five pound notes as I requested. I had him make them up into a solid parcel, and after that I handed him the reel of film together with the negative film, which was also in my briefcase. Then I took my departure and, because I felt pretty sure that I was being followed, I turned into a café for lunch. Once there I dodged down into the gent's toilet at the back, locked myself in, and from the briefcase took this old pair of trousers, this scarf, and this old plastic mackintosh. As you know they fold very flat, being of very light material. The hat was also in the case just to add to the effect. Since nobody followed me into the toilet — just as I'd hoped — it looked very much as though a different person came out. Also, before I came out, I put the briefcase inside the parcel with the money, and strung it all up again, carrying it inside my raincoat, which, since the raincoat is as you can see a raglan style — hangs very loosely and permits of hiding things beneath it, especially bulky articles. I left the café, went straight to the post office and there addressed the parcel of money, with the briefcase, to myself. It will be here tomorrow morning and I am perfectly sure that I have given whatever watchdogs were looking for me the complete slip. As to my normal clothes they are also in the parcel and I am hoping that the illusion will be that the mysterious Henry Brixton has disappeared from the face of the earth. Altogether a highly entertaining morning.'

'Was he awkward to handle?' Dick grinned.

'Not exactly awkward — more flabbergasted than anything else. And the delightful thing about this business is that there is no possible chance of reprisal.' Curtis gave the full details and then added: 'I more or less bluffed my way through the last part when he warned me what I'd get for having held him to ransom in this fashion. I don't know a bit about his stock market activities but I can very soon make it my business to do so if he begins to make himself awkward. I don't think he will for a moment and I for my part intend to keep to my part of the bargain and not make any more demands on him now he has paid the required amount. I suppose one might call that honor among thieves,' he finished, grinning.

'Well, as far as I can see,' Christine remarked, 'I just can't imagine Samuel T. letting things go like this. He knows you've got some kind of an invention that is of almost priceless value — especially to somebody with an unscrupulous mind — and I don't think he'll let you rest until he finds out what it is.'

'My dear girl he's got to let me rest,' Curtis retorted. 'He doesn't know my real name and he's never seen me before — and I'm perfectly sure that I haven't been traced since I disappeared in that café. From this day forward Henry

Brixton ceases to exist.'

'Until the next time?' Christine enquired.

'Next time?'

'Well certainly. When you find another victim you'll have to go and see him or her and use some kind of false name or other. The more times you do this kind of thing the more you'll get known.'

'Yes,' Curtis admitted. 'There is a certain amount of truth in that. But can you imagine these various victims discussing their many indiscretions with one another in order to know my identity? I can't, my darling sister, not by any stretch of imagination!'

'Well, at least we can be satisfied on one thing.' Dick said, smiling and rubbing his hands together, 'and that is, that the first deal has come off very successfully — or at least we shall consider it has done so when tomorrow we each count out our thirty thousand pounds. The next thing now, Curt, is for you to show Chris and I how this apparatus works and then we can get busy with our system of shifts.'

'Yes, fair enough,' Curtis acknowledged. 'Just let me get rid of these horrible clothes and get into something worthwhile and then I'll join you. Oh, have you had lunch yet?'

'Yes, we had it round about noon. There's nothing to stop us carrying straight on now and the sooner we get to know the intricacies of this apparatus the better.'

So the moment he had changed and freshened up Curtis went thoroughly into the task of acting as mentor to his sister and Dick, showing them by way of specifications and plans, together with actual demonstration, how this Z-ray mechanism worked. There were many details that he kept to himself — vital details indeed — without which the machine could not possibly function. Curtis was not the kind of man to give everything away in a sudden move of generosity, not even to his sister. By late evening the first lesson was completed but even yet Dick and Christine had quite a way to go before they became entirely proficient in the art of controlling the equipment

'Do you think it will be a good idea,' Dick enquired, politely yawning behind his hand as eleven o'clock that evening came round, 'if we had a look at Samuel T. Wernham and see if he's suffering from any hangover after your visiting him this morning?'

'I consider it a waste of juice,' Curtis replied, switching the mechanism off. 'Having gained all I need from Samuel T. I'm not in the least concerned with what he does or what hangovers he's got. All that interests me now is a fresh victim, and I wish that we hadn't got to rely on this damnable law of chance in order to find one. The trouble is that if they're spread out too long between good 'prospects' we'll not find our financial returns particularly high. The whole art of amassing money in a game like this is by doing it rapidly before someone gets brilliant enough to figure out what we're up to.'

'Why,' Christine asked sharply, 'do you think that is a possibility?'

'It is always a possibility, my darling sister — but a very remote one. For one thing this equipment uses a type of vibration that a normal detector — such as is used by the Metropolitan Police for trying to discover pirate television users — could never locate, and for another thing, the only ones likely to make trouble are those with whom we negotiate. And they, knowing what will happen if they say too much, are not likely to open their mouths very wide. No, I have the impression that we're sitting pretty — at the moment anyway, which seems as good a time as any to wrap things up for the day.'

Dick struggled out of his laboratory smock and reached down his jacket. 'I'm all anxiety to see how things work out tomorrow and whether the cash gets here all right.'

'Well of course it will get here,' Curtis exclaimed. 'There'll be one real big row with the post office if it doesn't.'

'And who will make the row?' Christine enquired. 'You? I can't see you going to the post office and saying that you put ninety-five thousand pounds into a parcel and want to know what's become of it! It would lead to too many enquiries.'

Curtis made an irritated gesture. 'Oh, what's the use of dragging up all sorts of unlikely prospects? Lets call it a day and start fresh tomorrow, I'm about all in!'

5

Mystery caller

The registered parcel arrived for Curtis towards the middle of the following morning. Immediately he, Christine and Dick called off their 'instruction course' concerning the Z-ray, and Curtis quickly snapped open the cords of the parcel and opened it out. In triumphant silence he stood looking at the wads of notes wrapped up in his clothes just as he had packed them the previous day.

'I suppose they're genuine?' Dick asked, dubiously.

'Most certainly they are. Samuel T. knows better than to try and give me dud notes.'

'Well if by any chance he was smart enough to do so,' Christine remarked, 'he's won the game for the simple reason that you've given him the positive and the negative proof and there's nothing else to go on.'

'Isn't there?' Curtis grinned. 'I took two copies of that negative, my dear girl. There's one in the safe just in case. I'm no fool, believe me. Anyway, lets settle ourselves to the delightful task of counting out these notes. Thirty thousand each. It's a long job, but I can't imagine anything more worthwhile. There's also another smart angle in getting these notes in cash: they don't have to be declared on an income tax return. I feel that the Government gets more than enough out of us already — it's time we had a chance to help ourselves.'

Christine and Dick gave each other a look then settled themselves down on either side of the table with Curtis in the middle. For some considerable time after this they were busy counting out wad after wad of notes until at last they had satisfied themselves that the ninety-five thousand was indeed there. And as far as they could tell the notes were absolutely genuine. At any rate, the bank could very soon verify it. If they were not . . .

'If they're not,' Curtis said slowly, as this thought returned to him, 'I wouldn't give much for Samuel T. Wernham's reputation by tomorrow morning.'

He glanced at his watch and then gave a whistle. It was nearly half past one.

'Best thing I can do is take one of these notes to the bank right away and get it checked,' he said.

'And what happens if they're marked?' Dick asked worriedly. 'I wouldn't put it past Samuel T. to have devised some system whereby when the notes are handed in again it will be possible to trace who's done it!'

'That is something we've got to risk, but personally in the time I gave him I don't see how he could possibly have had a marking system devised. No, I think he's playing the game on the level for his own sake.'

Curtis wasted no more time. He hurried into his jacket and left the laboratory. Christine and Dick sat looking at each other over the sea of Treasury notes, which they had stacked in front of them.

'This,' Christine said, sighing, an anxious look in her dark eyes, 'is the nearest thing to El Dorado I have ever known. If only I could reconcile this sudden wealth with my moral outlook I should be entirely happy — but unfortunately I can't.'

'Oh, just let things ride,' Dick grinned. 'Personally, I'm not going to raise any objection to receiving thirty thousand pounds as easily as this. All I want to do is to get that apparatus thoroughly learned so that I can start out hunting for myself!'

'So you've been bitten by the bug too?' Christine asked, sighing. 'You know, what annoys me about this whole thing is — the financial considerations aside — there is such tremendous uses to which this discovery could be put which could benefit mankind in general.'

'Well, that of course is just a nice girl's outlook,' Dick smiled. 'You want to benefit people right and left because you have something which they haven't. Believe me if you did try and benefit them all you'd get out of them would be an empty pocket and in the end probably a stack of insults. That's what usually happens when you try and help some-body else. The thing that people most appreciate is having to pay through the nose for everything that they get, then they think they've got something. The more I see of the way Curt handles things the more I realize that the ruthless attitude towards life is the right one. He's that rare combination — a brilliant scientist and a sound businessman.'

Christine nodded slowly, but she did not say anything. At the back of her mind she was wondering where this extraordi-nary — and even dangerous — business was going to end.

Before long Curtis returned, and when he did he was grinning cheerfully. He put his thumbs up significantly.

'This note is absolutely genuine, so I think we can take it for granted that the rest of them are. Nor was I asked to wait for a few moments whilst the manager had a few words with me. Everything in the garden is lovely, my sweet ones, and the indiscretions of Samuel T. Wernham has netted us the cool sum of thirty thousand pounds apiece. Now I think it is time we had lunch, then we can carry on again with the study of this apparatus. By this evening you ought both to be fairly proficient — at least proficient enough to keep the thing tuned in case we should happen on to some new and lucrative incident.'

But despite the fact that within three more days Dick and Christine had become quite expert in handling the apparatus, and a system of constant watches had been arranged, there came into the all-seeing range of the Eye no incident that was worth relating. Indeed, now that the original novelty had somewhat died away there came into the business a certain quality of deadly monotony. Sitting some six hours at a stretch before the screen and moving the ray promiscuously up and down the British Isles — for the moment it had been decided that the activities of the Z-ray should be encompassed within this area — was becoming distinctly boring. Nor was it improved when Curtis, always a man of action, began to rave impatiently at the lack of opportunity.

'If only we could devise some kind of system whereby we could pick up some particular thing,' he muttered, when two weeks of this fruitless searching had gone on, and the expenses bill for power was steadily mounting.

'Far as I can see,' Dick said, 'there doesn't seem to be any conceivable way of anticipating an event. To do that you would have to conquer time itself and leap ahead a certain distance. Then you'd know what to do.'

'Possibly even, my wonderful brother has decided how time can be conquered,' Christine remarked, dryly.

'There are limits even to your wonderful brother's brilliance,' Curtis retorted. 'This is one case where we're absolutely stuck and have to rely on something turning up. It's the damnable waiting that gets me down!' He stood thinking for a moment, then he gave a low chuckle.

Dick and Christine, who were both on duty at the same time on this particular occasion so that they would be able that evening to take time out together to go to a theatre, glanced at Curtis in surprise.

'Something amusing?' Dick enquired, interestedly, and Curtis turned to him.

'Well I think it is. Since we don't happen to alight on something that can make a financial return, there's one sure way of livening the monotony, and that is by *making* an opportunity!'

'By doing what?' Christine asked.

'I was just thinking of two particularly odious young men with whom I had the misfortune to associate when I was in the television business. They had no liking for me and very often made me extremely uncomfortable. I was just thinking — it might be a very good idea to find out something about each of their private lives and how they behave — some very unpleasant little secret — and see to it that each one knows the other's secret. I think that might cause a fearful amount of trouble between them, and if it got far enough it might amount to actual hostility, even murder! If I could get my hands on something like that I could charge quite a pleasant sum to keep the murderer's secret. They both had wealthy parents so I imagine that the proposition might be worth attempting.'

'You mean set them at each other's throats?' Christine asked, staring in amazement

'That is a very good way of describing it, my dear. Yes. It will probably take me quite a few weeks to investigate their activities and find something worthwhile on which to go, but at least it would be something to aim at. I believe I shall make my first attempt tonight when you two are at the theatre, and as soon as I get something worthwhile I shall go into action. There's no guarantee that I will, but it's worth a try.'

What Dick and Christine thought of his idea did not concern Curtis in the least. He had decided what he was going to do, and that evening he did it. Just how far he got he did not say when Christine and Dick returned from their evening out together, but there was something in his manner which seemed to suggest that he had gathered a good deal of information which he would turn to useful account later.

'I assume,' he asked, when Dick put on

his laboratory smock, 'that you are going to do your four hours on duty in spite of the fact that you have had hardly any rest today?'

'Definitely,' Dick agreed. 'I knew what I was doing when I said that I would take Chris out to the theatre tonight. We had to have some sort of a change. Sticking in here all the time is enough to drive one crazy. Yes, I'll do my four hours spell, and then it'll be Christine's turn, if that's okay with you, Chris?' He glanced across at her.

She nodded and turned back towards the doorway of the laboratory. 'I'll just go and see about some supper being fixed and then I'll get along to bed,' she announced. 'As soon as the four hours are up, Dick, don't hesitate to call me.'

'I've had my supper already,' Curtis said, 'so I may as well knock off right now. Call me within eight hours, and I'll carry on.'

'Was there anything worthwhile in your searching tonight?' Dick asked, settling himself before the apparatus.

Curtis paused in the doorway and

glanced back at him. 'Yes, I think there was to a great extent, but it will be quite some time before I can turn any of it to use. I found quite a decided pleasure in watching the private lives of two of the young men I hate most on this earth.'

With that he left the laboratory and closed the door sharply.

Dick settled down, stifled a yawn, and lighted a cigarette. It had been pleasurable to be out for the evening, especially with Christine, but it made the necessity of his spell of duty, now that he had returned, somewhat irksome.

At the beginning of this strange activity he and Christine had been to a certain extent impelled to zealous endeavor by the thought of the money they would make out of it: now they were becoming a little disappointed by the lack of opportunity, for neither of them had the quick-thinking brain of Curtis, by which they might manage to make opportunity out of nothing — or almost nothing. So the hours passed.

It was towards three o'clock in the

morning, his four-hour spell of the equipment nearly over, when Dick found that the casually directed Z-ray was wandering towards what looked to be a suspicious incident. During his four hours on duty he had moved the ray through most of the big cities of the country, exploring the dark alleyways, looking inside many of the homes in the hope of finding something interesting — but without result — and now he had come back to London itself.

At the moment the beam was moving down a quiet back street somewhere in the East of London, according to the checkpoint on the relief map. What arrested Dick's attention was the furtive way in which a heavily clothed man was moving down a dimly lighted street, pausing at length under one of the solitary street lamps. After a moment or two he was joined by another man, and they both glanced about them with the unmistakable air of men expecting trouble at any moment. Dick watched them for a moment or two, switched off the laboratory light in order to get a better view and then tuned in the fine focus that brought the two men into head-and-shoulders relief. There was certainly something suspicious about it all. A solemn conflab in a notoriously sordid part of the city might contain the seeds of something interesting, especially at the unearthly hour of three o'clock in the morning. After a while the sound of their voices came through, punctuated ever and again by the hooting of tugs on the nearby riverside.

'Everything set?' asked one of them. And Dick was not particularly concerned which one of them it was, though it seemed to him it was the taller of the two who had spoken.

'Yes, everything. Her old man's gone on to night duty and she's left alone. There's nothing to stop us from getting at the upstairs window by taking the back stairs, and finishing her. She knows far too much for comfort.'

Dick sat up in sudden alertness and increased the volume control. The two men looked about them again, then the smaller one continued speaking in a lowered voice:

131

'I had a bit of a job finding her address, but I managed to get it at last out of Charlie. It seems she's got an upstairs room at forty-seven Birch Street, and at the moment she's living there under the name of Annie Walker. There's no dog kept in the place, and the old boy and his wife downstairs are as deaf as posts so there's nothing to fear. Everything's quite easy. We can get in at the window, smother her cries, and finish her. It's the only way we can ever feel safe.'

'Right,' the taller one agreed. 'How far away is this Birch Street, anyway?'

'Oh, about a couple of miles, no more. I know all the short cuts, so let's be on our way.'

Dick sat intently in his chair and watched as the men moved out of the screen. Immediately he operated the controls and brought a full-length view of them into operation as they hurried down the dimly lighted street. At the same moment a voice spoke behind Dick's ear, and he gave a start.

'We've got to do something about this, Dick, and quickly.' He turned to see

Christine's serious face in the light from the instrument panel.

'You heard that?' he asked quickly.

'Yes, certainly. I came in quite a little while ago, but you were so intent upon the screen that I didn't disturb you. I woke up in time for once, ready to take my turn at the controls. That conversation there sounded to me very much like attempted murder.'

'Hardly attempted,' Dick corrected. 'It's going to be murder when they get to that address in Birch Street. This seems to me to be one way where the Z-ray can be of benefit. I don't know anything about this woman, Mrs. Walker, but I do know that two men are going to try and blot her out, therefore it's up to us to try and stop it.'

'Right,' Christine confirmed, her eyes bright. Without any further hesitation she strode across to the telephone and quickly dialed Scotland Yard.

Dick watched her, then he gave a sudden start. 'Take care what you're saying over the phone,' he warned. 'Don't give your name or address or anything at all, otherwise they'll want to know how on earth you know all about it.'

Christine nodded quickly. 'Leave it to me. Hello . . . Can I speak to the night sergeant in charge?' There was a brief pause then the heavy voice of the sergeant-in-charge came through clearly on the wire as Christine listened.

'I have just happened to hear a conversation which may mean nothing or something,' she said deliberately. 'Two men whose identities I do not know were discussing quite near to me — entirely unaware of it, of course — the fact that they were going to blot out, at least I think that was the term, a woman by the name of Annie Walker who is living in an upstairs room at forty-seven Birch Street. I heard of this information on the dockside, and one of the men said that it was two miles to Birch Street from where they were then. I leave it to you to work that out; all I am doing is giving you the warning. They've only just started off and have two miles to cover, so perhaps you will be in time to prevent whatever crime they are intending to commit.'

'Thank you very much, madam,' came the gravelly voice over the line. 'May I have your name and address please?'

For answer Christine lowered the phone slowly and cut off. She gave Dick an enquiring glance.

'Yes, that's okay,' he acknowledged. 'They can't possibly trace that. Nobody on a dial telephone can be traced when it's an automatic control. We'll probably be able to read in the morning paper exactly what has been happening.'

Christine gave a little sigh and came back towards the instrument. There was a faraway look in her eyes.

'You know, Dick, for the first time since this invention I feel somewhat happier,' she said slowly. 'It's such a wonderful device for preventing crime before it happens. If only it could always be directed in that channel. I'm not terribly interested in collecting money at the expense of other people's mistakes, but in an instance like this one with which we've just dealt I'd be willing to do twelve hours duty at a stretch in the hope that it might benefit some poor soul or save them a great deal of misery or injury.'

'Well said,' Dick murmured, 'but there still remains the merciless fact that we have to make money somehow, and the more of it the better. There also remains the fact that your brother is the owner and inventor of this apparatus, and what he says goes.'

With that Dick got to his feet from in front of the apparatus and stretched himself wearily. 'Well, Chris, it's up to you for the next four hours, then we'll have to give Curt a nudge. If, however, you should happen on any incident as interesting as the one we've just dealt with don't hesitate to let me know, and I'll be glad to assist if at all possible.'

'Rely on me,' Christine nodded. 'Things like that are about the only circumstance for which this instrument is really fitted.'

She seated herself where Dick had been, made herself comfortable and then prepared for her long vigil. Nothing happened during the period in which she was on duty, however, so towards seven o'clock she went to her brother's room, awakened him, and then retired to her own room to freshen up for the day's business.

It was during breakfast, which Christine and Dick had together since Curtis had to remain beside the machine on duty, that they gained the first hint of what had happened during the night. The news editor of the morning paper evidently did not consider the incident significant enough to warrant a large headline, but nonetheless a fair sized column had been devoted to it. The heading to the column ran:

MYSTERY CALL STOPS MURDER!

and then the column continued:

'In the early hours of this morning Scotland Yard received a call from an unknown woman, warning them of a potential murder. The name and address of the intended victim was given, and, thanks to prompt police action, the woman was saved from being attacked by two men. The two men were arrested as they entered the house where the woman was asleep, and they were taken in charge. The police are now anxious to trace the unknown third party whom they believe must have been connected with the two men and for some reason gave them away. Metropolitan Scotland Yard are now investigating the matter to the full.'

'Somehow,' Christine said, frowning as she read the column, 'I don't quite like the sound of this. They give the impression that I must have been one of the gang. All I was trying to do was to help!'

Dick sighed. 'It only bears out what I told you last night. Try and help anybody and sure enough you get yourself in a mess. It just doesn't work out. Maybe you should have kept quiet after all.'

'You didn't say that last night. You were as much for the idea as I was. After all, we couldn't sit there knowing that murder was intended and just let it be committed. It just wasn't to be thought of!' Christine pondered for a moment and then laid the newspaper aside.

'Oh well, I don't think that it

particularly matters. They can't ever trace me anyhow. As for my being a member of the gang, that's absolutely ridiculous.'

'True enough — we know that but the police don't, and at all costs you'd better keep that column away from where your brother can see it. I don't think he'll take kindly to the idea of your having involved yourself with Scotland Yard.'

Christine nodded gloomily, said no more and continued with her breakfast. When she and Dick had both finished they returned to the laboratory, both resolved to say nothing about their activities in the night, but to their inward consternation Curtis was reading a morning newspaper as he sat beside the televisor screen. Indeed he was dividing his attention between both. Christine noticed immediately that the paper he was reading was not the same one that she and Dick had read. Curtis indeed had a different political outlook to his sister, and therefore always read a newspaper of an entirely different 'colour' to hers.

'Well,' Dick asked cheerfully, 'anything happened?'

'That depends.' Curtis glanced up briefly — then he gave a look at the screen to make sure that he was not missing anything of importance — and continued — 'It seems to me from what I have just been reading in the newspaper that there's a matter of considerable interest which needs explaining. Take a look at this.'

He handed the newspaper across and waited in grim silence. The first thing that caught Christine and Dick's eyes was the big headlines on the front page. Evidently this particular news editor had considered his information worthy of a good spread. The headlines rose right out and said:

MYSTERY CALLER AVERTS TRAGEDY

Christine felt her heart racing a little more rapidly as she read the column that followed. It went into much greater detail than had her own paper and finished up with the poignant question:

'Was this unknown woman caller on the telephone a member of a criminal gang, who for her own reasons turned

140

the tables on her colleagues, or was she able by some unknown process to foresee an event which definitely would have taken place but for the prompt action of the police? Scotland Yard would be interested to hear from any observer or witness who might be able to throw light on this unusual circumstance. The position is extraordinary insofar that both men closely questioned stated positively that no one was anywhere near them or within earshot. There is no reason to suppose that these men are lying, since obviously their main objective would be to make things uncomfortable for the woman who had given them away. They assert, however, that no woman was ever connected with them except the one whom they were definitely intending to kill.'

'What,' Curtis asked, deliberately, 'does that sound like to you?'

Christine was silent as she handed the paper back, and Dick moved uncomfortably. Curtis, his mind still on his job, gave another glance at the screen, then his sharp brown eyes moved back to his sister.

'Well, Christine? What's the answer? Can it be that in the warm generosity of your heart you forgot all discretion and informed Scotland Yard about something that you happened to pick up on the Z-ray? It's either that or else someone has an apparatus identical to mine — which, I might add, I find extremely hard to credit.'

'No, it was my doing,' Christine said, with a defiant glance. 'It was Dick here who actually picked up the two men and heard all about them, but I happened to just come in at the same time and heard all that went on. He was as much in agreement as I was that the police should be informed, and save that woman's life.'

'How very touching,' Curtis commented, with an acid smile. 'And now you see the kind of mess that you've got us all into! Scotland Yard have got you fixed in their mind as one of the criminals who attempted the murder — and if I know anything about Scotland Yard they'll shift heaven and earth to try and find you.'

'Which they cannot do,' Dick pointed out. 'Chris rang them up on the laboratory phone, and since it's a dial instrument nobody will be able to trace where the call came from.'

'No I quite agree with that,' Curtis said, 'but the police have a habit, once they have an unknown somebody fixed in their minds, of pulling everybody to pieces until they've found that person. Things won't go at all well with you, Chris, if they ever do catch up on you. As you say, we're safe enough for the moment, but of all the damned tomfool, idiotic stunts — '

'I couldn't let that woman be murdered when I knew a way to stop it,' Christine interrupted. 'It's too late now, Curt, so it's no use you starting to make a row about it. If I came across a similar incident I'd do just the same again!'

Curtis sighed. 'I wonder why it has to be my lot to be saddled with a sister who considers herself chosen by Providence to look after the welfare of everybody else? Will you please try and get into your pin-headed brain, Chris, that if we make one mistake which gives away the whereabouts of this instrument — or our connections with it — our dreams of wealth will tumble into the dust. Henceforth, if you behold any murders or hear of any attempted murders just keep quiet and say nothing. Remember the old saying instead — 'Still tongue, wise head'.'

Christine did not say any more; indeed she had expected her brother to explode with far more violence than he had done. Possibly however he realized also that the saving grace lay in the dial telephone. Not by any method whatever could the police ever trace that, so the unknown woman who had spoken in the night had simply vanished from human ken.

'All right,' Curtis said after a while, 'you take over, Dick, since it's your turn and I'll go and grab some breakfast. You can do what you like, Chris, provided you don't feel tempted again to report the first villainous incident upon which you happen to alight.'

He gave a grim glance and turned and

left the laboratory. Without a word Dick sat down before the instrument to take his turn on duty. Christine stood beside him, her face drawn, her eyes troubled.

'So help me, Dick, I shan't be able to stand much more of this,' she exclaimed. 'Curtis is becoming absolutely intolerable, and all the money in the world doesn't make up for having to put up with him! Why don't we both quit and leave him to it?'

'As to that . . . ' Dick rubbed the back of his blond head slowly. 'It might be pretty foolish, you know, considering everything. We stand the chance of making a pile of money, and just because you happen to find your brother difficult to get on with I don't see passing that chance up. No I think we should stay on. And in any case I don't think Curt would let you go. He'd find something to make you stop. You and I are the only ones who know about this invention outside of him and he's not very likely to be willing to let us start talking outside.'

Christine was silent. She knew he was right. Both she and Dick were so deeply involved in this business now that any backward step was impossible.

'Tell you what though,' Dick said after a moment, 'there's one thing we can do. We can turn the Z-ray onto Scotland Yard, indeed straight into the office of the Metropolitan Division and see if we can pick up any information. We might be able to get an idea from that just how the land lies, or at least how much the Yard knows.'

He did not wait for Christine's assent. He immediately set the apparatus on the move, transferring the Z-ray from its wandering through the heart of London and concentrating it instead on that immense building on the Thames Embankment, the great new edifice where lay the headquarters of British Law and Order. This, however, was only the beginning of the search. They had to look in to department after department and listen to snatches of conversation before they finally happened on one which sounded reasonably appropriate The name on the glass paneled door of the office read 'Chief Inspector Halliday' and at the big desk, as the Z-ray penetrated further, there sat the broad-shouldered, heavy-faced man with iron gray hair deep in conversation with another man who, judging from his uniform, was a sergeant.

'That's the strangest thing ever, in regard to that woman Walker,' the Chief Inspector was saying, when the view faded in, and Dick gave Christine a quick, significant glance. 'We just can't let it stay like this, Harry. That unknown woman who sent the call during the night must have had something to do with the business otherwise she couldn't have known about it. The fact that those two bright birds say that no woman was connected with them we can take with a pinch of salt. Both of them are on our records as pretty desperate criminals and we can be reasonably sure that a woman will be mixed up somewhere with them. There always is a woman connected with that type of man. Since she was willing to turn informer against them she could probably give us a good deal of information about other matters in which they've been connected and about which, of course, they will not speak.'

The sergeant gave a shrug. 'I don't really see what we can do about it, sir. Not much hope of tracing anything on a dial telephone. We'll only get a lead if she ever speaks again.'

'Yes,' the Chief Inspector admitted, brooding. 'I suppose that is the answer, really. The whole thing indeed is one big puzzle. Why should two men defend the very woman who's given them away? For sure enough they'll be charged with attempted murder and they'll get the hell of a sentence for that. It just doesn't fit in with the normal psychology of a criminal, Harry — that's the trouble. The protection of an informer is about the last thing a criminal is ever willing to grant and in this case it isn't just one man who is doing the protecting it's both of them.'

'The fact remains, sir, there must have been a woman with them,' Harry said. stubbornly. 'In no other possible way could she have known what they intended.'

'My conclusion is that she must have had extraordinarily sharp ears,' the Chief Inspector mused. 'By their own confession the men spoke in very low voices and as far as they could see — and they are accustomed to looking for trouble around them — there was no woman or even anybody at all within earshot of them. It makes you think! Indeed it makes you wonder if that voice wasn't the voice of a ghost . . . '

Since after this the Chief Inspector turned his attention to other matters Dick swung the Z-ray away from Scotland Yard's mighty edifice on the Embankment, and again resumed the steady crawl through the byways and alleyways of the great city — looking, searching, hoping for the unusual which could by Curtis' ingenious methods be turned into a financial proposition.

Half an hour later Curtis returned into the laboratory and his expression was thoughtful. He looked rather surprised as he beheld both Christine and Dick at the instrument since it was Christine's turn off duty.

'The two love birds just can't bear to be parted from each other, I suppose?' he enquired cynically. 'Personally I shouldn't think any woman was worth losing sleep for. Well, anything interesting happened while I've been at breakfast?'

'Nothing,' Dick said flatly, satisfied himself that the investigation at Scotland Yard was nothing to do with Curtis.

'I have been giving a lot of thought to those two odious colleagues of mine that I mentioned yesterday,' Curtis continued, drawing up a chair and sitting down. 'Last night whilst you two were wasting your time at the theatre I investigated their private lives, as I said I would do. I made an interesting discovery concerning both of them.

'Just in case you have the inclination to warn one or the other of them what my intentions are I shall not let you know their names or their addresses. I shall simply refer to them as Mr. A. or Mr. B. Mr. A. is engaged in the by no means original occupation of keeping two homes going — in other words he has what one might term a spare time wife as well as his own. That in itself would be a useful thing to make capital out of, but I don't propose to do anything about that. What I do propose to do is — to go to work on

Mr. B. I long suspected whilst I was working beside him that as one of the chief radio designers he had more than one iron in the fire. Last night I was unfortunate enough to discover that he is trading some of his own firm's biggest radio secrets to a rival concern and making a very nice packet out of it as well. Not his own inventions, mark you, but those that are the work of the designing staff of the firm by which he is employed. It is his job to vet all these designs and of course the terms of his contract with the firm insists that he shall keep absolute confidence with his employers. He is going dead against this and selling the designs with modifications to the biggest rival firm there is.'

'Out of which,' Christine asked, 'you propose to make some more money?'

'Naturally. I must endeavor to check his dishonesty in the most painful way possible. I first thought that it would be a good idea to inform Mr. A. anonymously of Mr. B.'s indiscretions and set them at one another's throats. I would also, of course, have informed Mr. B. of Mr. A.'s indiscretions with his other wife. But being the men they are I think they would have come to terms and kept quiet about each other. That would have spoilt my little plan. So the thing to do is to secretly inform A. what B. is doing and unless I am entirely wrong in my judgment of his somewhat unscrupulous nature, he will immediately set to work to blackmail Mr. B. for all he's worth.'

'Then where do you come in with all this?' Dick asked, bluntly.

'I shall come in when Mr. B. can no longer bear being bled white and will blow his top. He is a fiercely impulsive man with an almost uncontrollable temper and if this goes on long enough he will probably endeavor to kill Mr. A., and that is when I will step in and collect. I know he can afford it because he has made a great deal of money out of the designs he has been selling — whereas Mr. A. has not made a great deal of money: his double life takes all the cash he can spare, therefore he's not worth my consideration.'

'Well, if that isn't deliberately making

trouble, I just don't know what is,' Christine exclaimed, disgusted. 'Curt, why on earth can't you — '

'Now don't you start again Chris!' There was bitterness in Curtis' dark eyes. 'You've bungled things enough already without trying to call me to account. Too many remarks out of you and I'll anonymously inform Scotland Yard that you are the woman they are looking for in connection with that business last night, and after that things will be mightily uncomfortable for you. Naturally I'd do it without involving myself: I'd see to that.'

'Oh, so that's how things stand now?' Dick asked, bitterly. 'You're using that business last night as a lever over Chris. Is that it?'

'That's it,' Curtis affirmed. 'If it has done nothing else it has at least gained for me the assurance that Chris here will do as she's told in future. Now you two take all the time out you want for the moment. I have several details to study out regarding Mr. A. and Mr. B. and I will need the televisor for them. Be ready to return to work at about two o'clock and that will give me the afternoon for relief.'

Since Curtis was the boss his orders had to be obeyed. Christine got up from the instrument and wandered out of the laboratory with Dick at her side. They reached the lounge before Dick spoke.

'Now you see what I meant when I said it would be difficult for you to escape. Curtis has got you all nicely taped up I'm afraid.'

'It certainly looks that way,' Christine admitted bitterly. 'In doing somebody a good turn I've got myself into a complete hobble. Great heavens, Dick, I wish to God I'd never seen this infernal Z-ray or had anything at all to do with it! The money in the bank doesn't compensate me in the slightest for the mental turmoil that is created.'

'You'll have to try and grin and bear it, that's all,' Dick said, putting an arm about her shoulders. 'Let's get out for a bit and get some fresh air — maybe we'll feel better then.'

6

Fatal provocation

Curtis Drew's studies of the two characters whom he enigmatically referred to as A. and B. covered a period of several days. What exactly he did during these days neither his sister nor Dick had the least idea. He did most of the work when they were either off duty together or they were catching up on some lost sleep. Neither of them asked any questions for they knew that they would not be answered. Indeed, ever since the incident that had saved the life of Annie Walker a certain air of mutual distrust had arisen. Curtis plainly did not any longer rely either on his sister or Dick Englefield, and they for their part were so inwardly nauseated by Curtis' ruthless tactics that they no longer cared for his company. The fact that he had made it plain what he would do to Christine if she dared to step out of the set-up was yet another cause of the bone of contention.

Surprisingly however, after he had spent two weeks of mysterious activity concerning A. and B., Curtis himself came out into the open one evening at a time when all three of them were assembled in the laboratory prior to breaking up into their normal shifts.

'You have doubtless been wondering what I have been doing with the two odious colleagues to whom I referred?' he asked, glancing from Dick to his sister.

'Wondering, yes,' Dick agreed, 'and that's about all. You've been tighter than an oyster since you first mentioned it.'

'With good reason. I wanted to be sure of what I was doing before I said anything definite. However, I seem to have more or less got things exactly as I want them. I told you some time ago what I'd discovered about A. and B., so accordingly I wrote A., anonymously, concerning B.'s activities. That certainly put the cat among the pigeons with a vengeance. Being precisely the fellow I thought he was, he immediately went to work to blackmail

156

B., and so far B. has paid up. But A., unlike me, doesn't know where to stop and he has kept on dunning B. for more money during these past few weeks. The result is that B. is about ready to do something unpleasant to this bloodsucker, who is sapping his financial vitality. I expect the crisis tonight — and I am hoping — knowing B.'s volatile temper — that it may end in crime. If so I've got things exactly as I want them. You two can either stay to witness the proceedings, or if you are at all squeamish, as you probably are, you can go out together and waste more time at the theatre. Whatever happens I've got work to do.'

'We're not going out anywhere,' Christine said coldly. 'We prefer to see what kind of monkey business you are up to. By this time we've become pretty well hardened to your way of doing things.'

Curtis shrugged. 'Please yourself . . . ' He sat down at the ever-operative instrument and adjusted the dials swiftly. Dick and Christine drew up chairs and proceeded to watch the screen.

By the time two hours had passed they

were both secretly wishing that they had taken Curtis' advice and not seen any of the performance enacted on the screen.

Through the two hours they followed character B from his quite comfortable home at the west end of the city and saw him visit the apartment of Mr. A. There was an exchange of money, high words floated through the loudspeaker and at last B. did the very thing that Curtis had anticipated. Losing his temper he whipped an automatic from his pocket and fired it three times with vicious satisfaction. Yet the instant he had done it he was obviously aware from his expression of the enormity of the crime that he had committed. He left the apartment hurriedly and the Z-ray followed him relentlessly until he reached his home. It was only at this point that Curtis switched off and sat back in his chair, smiling thoughtfully.

'What a wonderful judge of human nature I am,' he murmured after a moment or two. 'Good for Mr. B.! He did exactly what I thought he would. This lot means he hasn't an earthly chance of escaping me.'

'Did you take a film record of that scene?' Christine asked coldly. 'I didn't notice the camera in action if you did.'

'I used a different kind of camera this time,' Curtis told her, glancing round from his chair. 'I have embodied it inside the equipment itself. One touch of a button and it photographs and records everything without the need of my having to rely on either of you two to do the job. You see, since things have become a trifle strained between us I have a great deal of difficulty in placing any trust in your activities. You might quite easily fail to photograph an important scene sometime and lose us a great deal of money. I don't intend to take that chance — hence the reason for the concealed and ever-operative camera.'

'Since you've ceased to trust us,' Dick said sourly, 'why don't you give us a complete release from any connection with this business and you can collect any money you like on your own? We shan't say a word once we get outside; in fact we've got to the place where the whole thing damn' well disgusts us!'

Curtis got to his feet and came to where the two were seated, a sardonic smile on his thin face.

'As far as that goes, Dick, I do trust you, because I think you would be too big a fool to try and say anything once you left here — but I'm afraid I cannot trust my dear little sister. She might get a sudden attack of high morality and decide that what I am doing is not entirely ethical and in that mood she would be capable of anything. Even to informing Metropolitan Scotland Yard what I am up to. The fact that she might also be roped in as a witness for that murder case — or rather attempted murder case — would not concern her in the least if she felt that she was pursuing a very noble object. No, no matter how taut our relationship might become I don't intend to release either of you. You'll stay here for as long as it's good for you, but of course, if you're not anxious to receive any of the monies accruing from the invention that is up to you. I can make good use of whatever money is received.'

'All right, all right,' Christine said, with a weary shake of her head. 'Let it go, Curt. Since we have to stay beside you we might as well be as amenable as possible, but don't think that at the first chance that offers we wont make a dash for it!'

Curtis chuckled. 'I never saw two people so averse to making a pile of money in a perfectly simple way! You must be plain crazy, the pair of you. Anyhow, I've better things to do than try to work out the incomprehensible processes of your mind. The point to decide now is, how much do we charge Mr. B. for his indiscretion, and remember, this is a really big indiscretion this time! Nothing short of murder. A man should be willing to pay with everything he's got to save himself from the consequences of that!'

'We've had nothing to do with it,' Dick said. 'Why include us in the financial returns?'

'Because you're still partners in the scheme, that's why. And if anything should ever happen to this 'business' of ours to bring it to the notice of the authorities, I intend that you two shall be brought into it with me. For that reason you are entitled to be the recipients of all monies therefrom. Now, what price do we charge? I happen to know that Mr. B is a man of fair financial means — though he's certainly not a Samuel T. Wernham. I think, however, that he can comfortably afford sixty-five thousand pounds, which would be twenty thousand for each of us and the odd five thousand to put into the pool for later expenses. How does that strike you?'

'Up to you,' Christine said indifferently. 'I'd willingly pay you all my share for the chance to get out of this lot.'

'I am not going into that again.' Curtis said, stonily. 'Twenty thousand each it is, and the sooner I act the better. I'm going this evening to see what I can do.'

With that he turned to the laboratory doorway and then he hesitated. He came slowly back again to where Christine and Dick were still seated.

'It occurs to me that you two might like to look in on the proceedings,' he said slowly, 'and there will be nothing to stop you now since you know how the apparatus works. But it so happens that I have devised a foolproof locking system, which makes it impossible to use the apparatus unless you know the trick. You will be wondering why I have done that, I suppose?'

'Nothing that you do any more can surprise us,' Christine retorted.

'I have done it,' Curtis said, deliberately, 'so that neither of you can be stricken by a sudden fit of nobility. If during my absence you happen to alight on an incident like the Walker case I don't want you advertising freely that you know all about it. We got away with it once but we might never do so again. So that apparatus remains absolutely dead while I am not present.'

'Well in that case what the devil are we working in shifts for?' Dick asked, angrily. 'If you're going to lock the thing up every time you're not on duty there's no point in Christine and I working here at all. That's a mighty good reason for us getting out!'

'I am only concerned with the times I am not in the house,' Curtis replied, returning to the door again. 'When I am present here, even though I am in another room either sleeping or relaxing, you'll never know but what I might walk in at any moment and that in itself should be a sufficient deterrent. When I am out you will know that I cannot possibly walk in suddenly if you get a bright idea. See you later.'

With that he went out and shut the door sharply.

Christine and Dick looked at each other then Dick got to his feet and strode across to the instrument, switching it on in the way he had been instructed. Nothing happened; the control bulbs failed to light, and there was no humming in the generator. Whatever the negative system that Curtis had applied, it was working with extreme efficiency.

'This is about the limit,' Dick muttered, clenching his fists. 'And it also seems to me that Curt is defeating his own ends by doing this. While the thing's locked up ten to one something really important will happen that might be really useful.'

'To my mind,' Christine said, 'the whole thing is peculiarly illogical. If Curt is so anxious to keep us from recording any incident that he considers dangerous I cannot see why he shouldn't keep the instrument out of action whenever he is not present, whether he be in the house or not. Knowing Curt as I do I think he has some other reason for making the machine inoperative when he is outside the house. The only guess I can make is that he doesn't wish us to know the terms of the deal he makes with whoever his latest victim might be.'

'More bluntly put you mean that perhaps the financial terms he arranges are henceforth going to be more to his advantage than to ours?'

'Knowing Curt, yes.' Christine nodded slowly, then she shrugged. 'Not that it matters much anyway, because there's nothing we can do about it, but this whole beastly business is growing into such a circle of distrust life isn't worth living any more. No use having thousands in the bank and no peace of mind, is it?'

'Well, whatever the circumstances, it's money,' Dick said, pondering. 'And money's the one thing that nobody can do without. There must come an end to it finally, and when it does we should have enough cash beside us to be very comfortable indeed.'

With that he lighted a cigarette and relaxed beside the useless instrument, whilst Christine rose to her feet, yawned slightly and came over to him.

'I don't know what you're going to do, Dick, I'm going to bed. For one thing I'm tired and for another I don't see the point in staying up to listen to whatever revolting story Curt has to tell of his deal with a murderer. The fact that he has incited one man to kill another so that he can make a financial gain is about the last straw as far as I am concerned. And I'm still not sure that I won't walk out before I've finished and let him do his damnedest!'

'We'll discuss that again, if things get entirely beyond the pale,' Dick said. 'Meantime, you go to bed and get some rest. I'll stay and see what Curt has to say when he comes back.'

Christine nodded, turned, and left the laboratory . . .

It was nearly half-past twelve when Curtis finally returned — and there was something about his expression that showed he was not particularly satisfied about the way things had gone. Dick looked up and gave him a moody glance.

'Well, manage to get your blood money?' he enquired.

'Not a sausage.' Curtis pulled off his coat and hat and threw them on a nearby chair. Then he stood grimly thinking, his hands plunged in his trouser pockets.

'You mean he didn't cough up?' Dick asked in surprise. 'Why was that? Because you didn't take a film reel with you? I noticed that you didn't take anything out of this machine here.'

'No. I was going to use that tomorrow as my proof and make the preliminary arrangements tonight. But things have gone completely wrong. When I got to B.'s house I noticed that the garage lights were still on along with the headlights of his car so I assumed, naturally, that he had just driven into the garage and if I could catch him it would make things much more simple than having to deal with him in his house. I went into the garage and saw him inside the car. I thought perhaps he was having some kind of ignition trouble or something, but I discovered after a moment or two that he was dead!'

'Then what?' Dick asked, quietly.

'I found,' Curtis continued, 'that he had shot himself through the head with the same automatic with which he had killed A. So I obviously don't get any money out of him . . . The point that is worrying me is that I was seen entering his house, though of course not quite close enough to be easily identifiable as far as face is concerned, by a group of teenagers who were chatting about some rubbish or other under the street lamp which is just outside Mr. B.'s house. They certainly saw me enter for they stopped talking and watched me in the way that young people have. Now it is quite conceivable that, although I was wearing gloves, I may have left many marks inside B.'s car, for I took my gloves off as I reached inside to examine him, not knowing then that he was dead and thinking that he'd merely fainted. As far as I know I've cleaned up all the prints I might have left behind, but there remains the unpleasant thought that there still may be some. When I realized the situation I got out quick. It could very easily look as though I had walked into that garage and put an end to him. And, if the police ever get far enough to pin anything on to my fingerprints, they will also discover that I had never liked Mr. B. when I had been working beside him in the radio business.'

Dick's serious face suddenly broke into a grim smile, and presently the smile changed into a laugh.

'That,' he said, gasping for breath, 'is about the funniest thing that I ever heard of, and serve you damn' well right! You got those two men at each other's throats, just to get money out of one of them, and he goes and commits suicide and you're straight in line for getting the blame for murdering him. If that isn't a good example of the biter bit, I don't know what is!'

Curtis sat down deliberately and lighted a cigarette, his thoughts obviously miles away. In fact, so many miles away he took no notice of Dick's hilarity.

'The more I come to think of it,' he said slowly, 'the less chance I can see of my being involved in this business. I had no actual connection with B. so the police will find it practically impossible to trace anything. And even if they do find fingerprints they cannot take any of mine without first making a charge and they'll have to be mighty sure before they do that. As for the babbling teenagers under the street lamp, I don't suppose they'll ever come into it and if they do it's not very likely that the police will place much credence on their testimony. No, I think the situation is comfortable enough but it's damned annoying to be cheated out of the money when I had got everything so nicely arranged.'

'What about the anonymous letter that

you wrote to A?' Dick enquired, pondering. 'Do you know whether he destroyed that or not or can the police get hold of it?'

'I've not the slightest idea what he did with it, but I think when things come to be looked into, the police will assume that it was A. who killed B. because they were both involved and there was blackmail to boot.'

Dick shook his head, for once revealing a surprising flash of sagacity. 'I shouldn't place too much store on that if I were you, Curt. The police surgeon when he comes to examine them will very soon prove that A. died before B., therefore he couldn't possibly have shot him. It must have been someone else. I only hope that that anonymous letter that you wrote does not in any way get traced. If it does you are going to be in a damned uncomfortable spot. Don't think that I'm worrying about you in this,' Dick went on, getting to his feet, 'it's Christine and myself I'm thinking of. I haven't forgotten that you said whatever happened in this business I'm going to be dragged in it too.

I want to know just how likely it is that you might suddenly find yourself in jail.'

'That anonymous letter was posted in the centre of London,' Curtis replied, blowing a smoke ring into the air. 'Since tens of thousands of people could have posted that letter there cannot possibly be any way of tracing it back to me . . . No, I'm entirely confident that nothing can possibly incriminate me, so, having failed on this particular count, where I felt sure that I could have netted a good few thousand, I might as well turn my attention to something else. Incidentally, I have something lined up which I think would really pay off — and in very big money too!'

'Another industrialist, perhaps?' Dick questioned, but Curtis shook his head.

'No, not an industrialist. Nothing less than the Jetway Atomic Corporation. According to the papers and all the other information that I have been able to dig up lately, it seems they are engaged on the design of a revolutionary aircraft. It will probably be the first plane able to travel beyond the very limits of the atmosphere

— into space, in fact — and of course, everything in connection with it is a closely guarded secret. Such an aircraft would revolutionize international travel, by cutting down on the journey time. Therefore it seems to me that if I take a cine film of the plans for this super-plane and everything else that I can gather concerning it and then pass them on to a foreign Atomic Corporation, there ought to be a great deal of money in it.'

Dick smiled coldly. 'From murder to spying, eh? In one easy stride! You're slipping, Curt!'

'That isn't funny,' Curtis said. 'I know where I can make the necessary contact with a foreign power and I'm also sure that that foreign power will pay a very big sum indeed. I know that most spies get very little for the information they obtain, but in this instance it won't be just a part of an idea; it will be the entire construction of an absolutely revolutionary aircraft. Of course, come to think of it, I might get hold of all the necessary information and try and construct such a craft myself. I shall very soon have enough money to be able to stand the racket of the engineering necessary for such a project . . . '

Curtis thought this one out for a moment or two and then shook his head. 'No, come to think of it, that might be much too risky. Far better to make a sale to a foreign power and add to my bank account. That's the only thing that I'm interested in at the moment. Adding money to what money I have.'

'And do Christine and I come into this as far as the clean-up is concerned?'

'Naturally. I shall need your help in many things when I start my examination of the Jetway Corporation.'

There was silence for a moment. Curt stubbed out his cigarette, then he got to his feet and stood thinking.

'There's a question I'd like to ask you,' Dick said, eyeing him steadily.

'Go ahead, but don't make it a damned awkward one. I'm too tired to bother.'

'It's this: Have you deliberately arranged a cut-out on this equipment so that nei-ther Christine nor I can see what kind of a financial deal you make at the other end?'

Curtis grinned. 'That sounds exactly like my dear little sister. I bet the idea came from her! The damned funny part of it is that it's right! I give you two a figure but what I arrange at the other end is entirely my own affair. If you've agreed to a certain sum — well, that's that! If I can get more than I originally intended — which I certainly didn't with Samuel T. Wernham, I can assure you — all the better for me. After all, I am the inventor and owner of this apparatus and it is only my magnanimity that makes me let you and Christine have any money at all. You should feel grateful, not try and find fault.'

'There was a time,' Dick said, slowly, 'when I admired you, Curt. I thought you were an extremely brilliant man both in science and in business. I still believe that you are brilliant as far as science is concerned, but your business is of the rottenest kind! In fact, not to put too fine a point on it, I think you're nothing better than a dirty-minded devil!'

'I do believe,' Curtis said, musing, 'that

Christine would like to call me that many a time, but being for some reason of a highly refined nature she just contents herself with glacial looks. I'm glad to know what you think of me, Dick, because it makes me all the more determined to see that you and Christine go down with me if there should ever come a crash. You won't get away with a statement like that without me remembering it for a very long time . . . '

The two men stood looking at each other for a moment, then at last Dick turned away in disgust.

'I'm going to get some sleep,' he said briefly. 'I should have had my head examined when I decided to come and live here so as to keep constantly on the job. Before, I did at least have the chance of some fresh air before I got home. As it is, I've got to live in this stinking atmosphere for an indefinite period. However, if the police of Metropolitan Scotland Yard are half as smart as they think they are perhaps the indefinite period will not be so long as I fear.'

With that Dick went out and slammed

the laboratory door. Curtis compressed his lips and turned to the equipment, stifling a yawn as he did so. It was perfectly plain that the night's session would have to be run entirely by him, so it might as well be turned to advantage. Getting up he went to the nearby shelf, mixed himself a glass of restorative, drank it, and then returned to his chair before the instrument panel.

7

Baited trap

Switching on Curtis set the Z-ray in action once more, and that relentless probe flashed invisibly through the night until at last it had centralized itself upon the vast acreage of squat buildings covered by the Jetway Atomic Corporation. Right through the electrified enclosures and the hoards of guards went the Z-ray, finally centering upon the gigantic laboratory with which Curtis was already familiar. It was in here, hidden from the world, that the first of the gigantic airliners intended with the capability of flight into outer space was being constructed. At least, it was the first of the British aircraft: what was happening in other countries was not Curtis' concern at the moment. He knew full well where he could trade his secrets and that was all that counted. Even he did not fully realize himself the lengths to which he was now going. From dealing with an immoral tycoon to stealing the secret of the most hush-hush project in British aviation history was a gigantic stride, and a dangerous one. But so confident was he of his security, despite the jolt he had received that evening after the suicide of Mr. B,, he carried out the plan which he had already devised.

Adjusting the Z-ray and setting into action the re-loaded cine camera within the apparatus, he proceeded to make a careful study of the huge aircraft around which mechanics and technicians were working with calm efficiency. The sound through the speakers was that of the various machines at work — the grinding and polishing, wiring and screwing, sawing and riveting. Here the night shift was hard at work, entirely unaware that an ubiquitous Eye was taking in and photographing every detail and recording also all the corresponding sounds. It was not a necessity at this point that the sound should be recorded, but knowing where he intended to sell this film record, Curtis considered that perhaps the sound might be an added help to the foreign engineers when they came to see the film through.

Altogether Curtis spent nearly an hour making extremely fine focus close-ups of the craft and then passing through its metal walls into the interior and recording every detail of the infinitely complicated switchboards. Here was spying on the grand scale. No blueprint or photostat ever stolen by an espionage agent could possibly have the wealth of information and photographic accuracy that was being stored here. And, when he felt that he had gathered all the necessary details of the actual aircraft itself, Curtis sent the Z-ray speeding through the wealth of low-buildings until he came to the design rooms. Here again the night staff was at work, busy on the plans of the revolutionary aircraft, and maneuvering the Z-ray with all the skill he could muster Curtis succeeded by degrees in getting a complete record of all the necessary specifications and designs, together with the secret of the extremely powerful atomic motor.

When at last his task was finished he

found that it was pretty nearly four in the morning and he was stiff with cramp from being seated so long in one position. Yawning and wincing he struggled to his feet, switched off the apparatus and lighted a cigarette. Smoking pensively he strolled up and down the laboratory to restore circulation of his deadened limbs and then thinking to himself he removed the several reels of films which had been exposed in the camera, each one having automatically slipped into place as its predecessor had reached its finish.

'Lovely,' Curtis murmured, as he surveyed the array on the bench in front of him. 'It is even possible after this that no more investigations will be necessary. This lot should be worth a fortune in itself.'

Curtis did not stay much longer in the laboratory. He wrapped up the films carefully in a sealed package, put it in the safe, and then departed for some much needed sleep.

He did not explain the following morning at breakfast what he intended doing, merely saying to Christine and

Dick that he had important work to attend to and that they could do exactly as they pleased.

'And, of course, the machine is all locked up I suppose?' Dick asked.

'Whilst I am out of the house, yes. That I have decided to make an unvarying rule.'

'This whole situation is ridiculous,' Christine said, hotly.

Curtis gave his cold smile. 'Ridiculous it may be, my dear, but some of the work that I did during the night ought to pay off an extremely high dividend. In this particular instance I'm not going to suggest that we decide a price between us: you will take exactly what I decide to give you and be glad of it.'

'Which means, I suppose,' Dick asked, 'that you spent the night stealing secrets from the Jetway Atomic Corporation?'

Christine gave a start. 'The Jetway! Great Heavens! Curt, you don't mean to say that you — '

'I mean to say,' Curt interrupted deliberately, 'that I have been photographing in detail the first secret passenger airliner

182

capable of reducing its travel time by going into outer space. I have every possible detail that foreign engineers could wish to know, together with close-up photographs of the blueprints and drawings appertaining thereto. I am going out today to make special contact with the agents concerned with whom I have been in touch for a long time against such a chance as this. And I venture to think that the amount I ought to clean up from a proposition of this nature will make it unnecessary to search for fresh victims for a very long time. So, once this deal is completed it will leave you two more or less free to concentrate on each other — though heaven knows why you should. At the moment you have made thirty thousand pounds apiece for hardly any work. I am prepared to be magnanimous enough to make it up to one hundred thousand each for both of you, after which we'll come to some arrangement regarding the parting of the ways. It's becoming perfectly obvious that we can't continue beside each other whilst such friction exists. For the time being just stay as you are and leave me to handle everything else.'

In the face of this there was nothing more to be said as far as Christine and Dick were concerned, but the moment Curtis had left the house Dick got to his feet in sudden resolve and looked at Christine determinedly.

'I'm not going to be treated like a child any more,' he declared flatly. 'Since we're tangled up with this Z-ray and know its enormous possibilities — I'm talking of the benefits it can bring in this particular instance — I think it's about time we went to work to make it useable for ourselves. Curtis may be something of a magician as far as electrical things are concerned, but whatever system he's used to make that apparatus inoperative it ought to be capable of being discovered. Now he's out of the way we've a good chance to see if we can locate the reason for the apparatus not working. Are you game to come along?'

'More than,' Christine agreed, getting to her feet quickly. 'Indeed, we might go one better than that since the time doesn't seem far distant when we get thrown out of here. We may as well take with us a working knowledge of how the Z-ray operates. I don't fancy leaving Curt behind with all the information. Even though he made all the actual apparatus it was my suggestion in the first place and you accidentally falling against the machine that brought the whole thing into operation. We're entitled to some share in all that, surely?'

Wasting no further time talking they hurried into the laboratory and Dick immediately set to work to make a thorough study of the equipment. Christine did what she could to help but her scientific knowledge was woefully limited and finally she contented herself with doing whatever Dick asked, and left the more difficult task of sorting out the details entirely to him.

At the end of an hour of investigation, during which he had made a complete analysis of the various cables and all the switches connected thereto, he turned to Christine and gave a shrug.

'The only way to try and get anything here is to take the front panel off,' he decided. 'The best thing you can do is keep a watch on the front of the house and if you see Curt coming back let me know immediately. I'll get the panel together again if it's at all possible. The foolproof system which he has devised along with the camera arrangements is somewhere inside the main controlling unit and we're never going to get to know anything until we get the front off.'

Christine looked somewhat aghast, knowing full well what would happen if her brother did return in the midst of the proceedings, but nevertheless she moved across to the laboratory window and there sat on the narrow ledge, keeping her attention fixed on the front of the house in case of a sudden emergency.

Immediately Dick went to work on the panel and within ten minutes he had managed to remove it. After that the task was not particularly difficult. He was by no means a scientific man nor even a brainy one, but even he didn't have much difficulty in realizing that the make-and-break switch in the main cable, cunningly connected to an outer dunning switch, was the method by which Curtis was able to make the machine inoperative. Perfectly simple and once found anything but foolproof. Dick gave a grin to himself, examined the fittings where the camera was attached, and then turned to Christine as, for a moment, she moved away from the window.

'There it is,' Dick said, spreading his hands. 'The simplest gadget in the world when you know which is the right one on the main panel. Nothing now but to put the whole panel back again and in future when your brother switches off, I, or you, will be perfectly able to switch on again at any moment we choose. Come to think of it there wasn't any other method he could have used outside of the main parts. And that would have entailed the difficulty of putting it back again whenever he wanted to go to work. Anyhow, from here on, we'll no longer be in the position of being like little schoolchildren, being told what to do by our teacher.'

To put the panel back again was a simple job and it was easily accomplished, without any sign of Curtis having returned. Indeed, he did not come back until towards four in the afternoon and when he did so he had only an empty briefcase with him and no sign of the film reels with which he had departed. Christine and Dick, both in the lounge, gave him a significant glance as he came in. He eyed them for a moment and then gave his slow, sardonic smile.

'You're all eagerness to know what happened,' he said, 'so why on earth don't you say so? Or better still, I can save you the trouble of asking questions and tell you that the deal went through. In fact, the whole thing couldn't have been easier. Within a day or two I shall be receiving a cheque — for the sum agreed upon and when that happens I'll see that you two get your due.'

'So in this instance you're risking a cheque?' Dick enquired.

'It's not a case of a risk,' Curtis replied calmly. 'The whole thing is done through an English bank in a perfectly legitimate way — or at least, it would appear so to the authorities. After all, I'm not the only person in England doing a foreign transaction. In a case like this the matter could not be handled in any other way.'

'Of all the risks you've taken this is definitely about the biggest. The Jetway Atomic Corporation is hardly likely to take things lying down when they discover that their most cherished secrets have passed into the hands of a foreign power.'

'A fact of which I am perfectly aware, my darling sister. To gain the big prizes in this life, however, you have to take the biggest risks. And after the failure of my deal last night I simply had to do something to — er — recover my losses, if I might put it that way.'

'Failure? Last night?' Christine looked surprised. 'You mean the deal that you had between A. and B., as you called them. Why, did it fall through?'

Curtis looked in surprise at Dick. 'It surprises me, Dick, that you haven't told her all about it by now.'

'No, I didn't tell her anything,' Dick

growled. 'The whole thing's too damned sordid.'

'There are times,' Curtis said, 'when I think that you two spend your time absolutely looking for the sordid. Well, Christine, you may as well have the facts . . . '

And Curt gave them to her in detail. At the end of the story Christine was looking even more alarmed than she had before.

'Then it means that if police investigation is carried through to its logical conclusion, they might possibly start suspecting you?'

'Every chance of it,' Curtis agreed, 'but I don't propose worrying myself about that until there's real necessity. My concern right now is to get this atomic deal of mine completed and then we can discuss on what terms we will part with each other's company. I shall be quite glad to be able to pursue my own career without constant questioning glances from darling little sister there.'

'Does this mean, then, that you don't intend to go any further with the Z-ray?' Dick asked. 'Does that mean that you've had enough victims for the time being?'

Curtis grinned. 'I doubt if one could ever have enough victims. But answering your question, yes. I am not investigating anything further for the moment. Indeed, when I do so again, I hope that I shall be doing it alone and that you two will be over the hills and far away — married possibly, you poor devils.'

With that he turned and left the room, smiling enigmatically to himself as he went.

'I'd give anything to know just how much he's made out of this deal,' Dick muttered giving Christine a grim look. 'I wouldn't wonder if it doesn't run into the millions.'

'Millions or pennies, it's all the same to me,' Christine retorted. 'The sooner he gets the whole thing done with and let's us go the better. What I'm wondering is, why you didn't tell me about that business last night with A. and B.'

'I didn't think it signified, and there was no point in adding to your worries by letting you think that Curt might yet be accused of a murder that he hasn't committed.'

'Hasn't committed!' Christine echoed scornfully. 'You come to think it over, Dick, and you'll see that he's committed two murders already, or rather one murder and caused one suicide. It's A. and B. I'm talking about. That would never have happened but for Curt. There's no getting away from the fact that even though he is my own brother he's rotten — right through.'

★　★　★

The one thing that Curtis Drew, with all his prescience, could never have foreseen was the crashing of an airliner in the Southern Alps on its way back across Europe from London airport. Not that the crashing of an airliner was anything new, but in this instance it carried for Curtis a vast significance. How great a significance he only knew the following morning when the information concerning the crash hit the headlines of the media. He, Christine, and Dick were breakfasting together, hardly exchanging any words — indeed, Curtis was absorbed in his newspaper — when suddenly he gave such an immense gasp of consternation that even Dick was startled for the moment.

'What's gone wrong now?' Christine asked, dryly. 'Metropolitan Scotland Yard catching up on you or something?'

Curtis didn't answer. He lowered the paper and stared fixedly in front of him for a moment, then he raised the paper and stared at it again.

'It's unbelievable,' he muttered. 'This sort of bad luck couldn't happen twice on the run. It just isn't possible!'

'Oh, what are you rambling about?' Dick asked, impatiently.

'Just this . . . The night airliner from London to Siberia crashed last night in the Southern Alps. A list of the passengers is announced in the papers here. Among them is Doctor Conrad Axel, a celebrated physicist. That doesn't mean anything to you, but it means a heck of a lot to me. Axel was the man to whom I sold the plans of the new airliner with space capability.'

'You mean he's been killed?' Christine asked blankly.

'Yes, along with fifty-seven other people. It's the same sort of filthy bad luck that dunned me when A. and B. got wiped out. That's the second proposition gone up in smoke. What makes it worse,' Curtis continued, looking genuinely worried for once in his life, 'is that Axel's briefcase has been found and in it are the films which I gave him. At least it says 'films of international importance' — and I know very well what that means.'

There was a grim silence in the room for a moment or two, then getting a hold on himself again, Curtis said:

'Well, even if they have found the films, they can't accuse me of anything. It will obviously look as though Doctor Axel was a spy and that will be the end of that. And it's also the end of the deal I made with him. The only thing to do now is to try and contact some other agent who . . . '

'You can't do that,' Christine pointed out. 'Now these plans have become common property, both of the European police and of Doctor Axel, you don't suppose any other agent would touch them, do you? No, Curt, you've lost that deal completely, like you did with A. and B. I think that the sooner you come to your senses and use the Z-ray for something beneficial, the better for all of us.'

'This is damnable,' Curt whispered. 'Nothing else but damnable! The best thing to do is to lie low as long as possible and see what happens. I still don't see how there can possibly be any connection with me. When things have quieted down a bit we shall really have to start looking for a victim who is worthwhile. I thought I'd made enough there to be able to clean up everything. Now it looks as though we'll have to start all over again. I can imagine you two feeling wonderfully pleased about that,' he finished sardonically.

'The only thing worrying us,' Dick said, 'is the same thing that's been on our minds all along. Namely, that if you go down in chaos and ruin, so do we. We haven't done anything to deserve it whereas you have.'

'That's a matter of opinion,' Curtis retorted.

He got up from the table then lounged from the room, his brow troubled. The door closed.

'This,' Dick said, sighing, 'is a particularly unpleasant situation. In fact, your brother's right on the edge of a volcano. The best thing he could do would be to destroy all that apparatus and try and bluff his way out of any trouble if it ever comes his way. The only point that may save the situation is that the Atomic people cannot possibly know how those plans were taken.'

In this observation Dick was undoubtedly correct, but of course, the moment that the news of the drawings and the plans reached M.I.5 in Metropolitan Scotland Yard from European Police Headquarters, many moves began to be made behind the scenes. The Jetway Atomic Corporation suddenly found itself in the midst of the most intensive investigation ever known, but of course, there was not the slightest evidence to show how those extraordinary clear movie reels had been taken, nor after the intense interrogation of the various employees did there seem to be a single one of them who could be directly accused as being the guilty party. It was quite one of the most baffling problems against which M.I.5 had ever thrown their resources. Technically indeed, Curtis Drew would have been entirely safe except that a certain financier, Samuel T. Wernham to be precise, was more than interested in the sudden astounding problem that was confronting the authorities. Indeed he had good reason to be interested insofar that he was one of the Governing Directors of the Corporation itself and therefore more or less locked up in its interests.

Immediately following the investigations of M.I.5 he called a conference of his fellow directors and to them addressed perhaps the strangest speech ever.

'I believe, gentlemen,' he said quietly, 'that this atomic plant has been at the mercy of an extremely clever scientist. Not necessarily one who understands atomic secrets, or one who could duplicate this advanced airliner which is under construction — but one who has the scientific knowledge of how to pierce closed doors and solid walls.'

'Sounds impossible to me,' one of the directors commented, chewing his cigar.

'That's what I thought in the first place — but to cut a long story short,' Samuel T. continued, 'I recently committed an indiscretion in my private life, which I felt absolutely sure was known only to me and the other party concerned. You understand?' He gave his big grin.

The assembled men nodded and looked at each other knowingly.

'Imagine my surprise, then,' Samuel T. continued, 'when the day after this indiscretion, I was visited by a man who called himself Henry Brixton. He held me up to ransom for the sum of ninety-five thousand pounds as the price of his silence. And in return for that sum he gave me a film and a negative in sound that had recorded the whole incident of which I have spoken. Doesn't it seem to you, gentlemen, that there is a parallel between that and this business at the atomic plant? There is also another matter which may or may not be linked with this, and that is the unusual case of the Walker woman. I don't know whether you read it in the Press or not but I was very deeply interested in it — insofar that it appeared two criminals discussed together in low tones the murder of a woman, and unwittingly gave her name and address, and this conversation was overheard by somebody entirely invisible, and the potential murder target was warned in time to be saved from disaster. That again seems to me to point to some scientific type of equipment, which was able to know of the event without anybody actually being present on the spot. I tell you, gentlemen, that somewhere, somebody has a deadly scientific instrument — some kind of Eye and Ear which can see into our private lives, and at any moment can hold us to ransom, even as I was.'

There was a sober silence. Nobody argued with Samuel T. Wernham — not because he was Samuel T. but because the proposition he had set forth, however fantastic, was the only one which seemed to fit the case. M.I.5 had definitely proven that no one in the ordinary way had been responsible for the theft of those valuable plans and sketches. Nor could anybody have possibly recorded a film in sound of the revolutionary airliner in the process of construction.

'Well,' one of the directors asked presently, 'what do you suggest should be done? If your belief is correct, S.T., the only thing to do is to inform the police. And what have we to go on? Nothing but your information about this man Henry Brixton. Have you never heard anything from him since?'

'Nothing at all. I even endeavored to have him traced, but it was completely useless. He gave my man the slip completely. As to his appearance, well — I have a very good idea of that, of course. He is medium-sized, lean featured, dark eyes with an habitually sardonic expression. Undoubtedly a man of considerable intelligence and, in his way, quite a good businessman. I have no more description of him than that and since it would fit thousands of men in London it perhaps doesn't help us much.'

'It might help the police,' another of the directors observed. 'I think we should inform Metropolitan Scotland Yard that — '

'Not if I know it,' Samuel T. interrupted. 'Doesn't it occur to you that if I inform Metropolitan Scotland Yard about this business they'll start enquiring into everything I've ever done in order to try and find out what Henry Brixton's reason was for blackmailing me as he did? Besides, gentlemen, since I can talk freely here, does it not occur to you that if we can get our hands on an invention like that we could extend our power immeasurably? Indeed, I tried to make such a bargain with this Henry Brixton, only — wise man! — he wasn't having any. I was even prepared to offer him millions there and then for the secret because I felt sure, and he as good as admitted it, that he possesses some mysterious scientific Eye the like of which has never been seen before.

'No: what I do suggest — with your connivance of course — is that I employ several of my own men to look into this matter and also use my chain of newspapers to try and further the investigation. I will describe Brixton's appearance to a skilled artist and have him draw a picture of him for publication in my papers. We can then ask the world in general: 'Do you know this man?' We might add an essentially modern flavor by adding headlines something on the lines of — 'Are other eyes watching us?'.'

'And what do you think will emerge from a campaign like that?' one of the men enquired, thinking.

'My guess is this,' Samuel T. replied slowly. 'Henry Brixton, wherever he may be, will not be aware that I am the owner of the newspaper which is publishing this news for the simple reason that the name of the proprietor does not appear in the newspaper itself. He will undoubtedly feel that the net is closing in around him and unless I am entirely ignorant of psychology, he might try and contact me in the hope that I might buy out his invention for the price I originally named, before it is too late. By that means it would automatically shift the blame to me, or so he will think, and be a considerable sum the richer when and if the police finally catch up on him. I shall obtain the instrument that I require and I will see that it is kept out of sight long enough for the police to forget all about it. Later we can use it to our own advantage. At any rate,' Samuel T. finished, 'I am sure it is worth a try and I think Henderson is the best man to handle this job.'

That his fellow directors would acquiesce to his scheme Samuel T. Wernham knew full well — and they did. Accordingly the quiet-voiced but intensely thorough Henderson was immediately given all the details and since he had handled many of Samuel T.'s more difficult cases in the past he was absolutely assured that he would be able to handle this one.

'I might even make a suggestion, sir,' he commented thoughtfully, when that evening Samuel T. had given him the details in his library. 'How would it be if these articles were written under my own name of Henderson and then Henry

Brixton, if he feels so inclined, will make every possible move to try and contact me? If he does I shall then be able to put him in touch with you and the deal will be completed in exactly the way you want it. It's no use having this type of newspaper article written by an apparent staff reporter, for that's the kind of person that Henry Brixton would never try and contact. He mightn't come far enough out into the open to try and contact you, either.'

'Yes,' Samuel T. agreed, after thinking for a moment or two, 'that's quite a logical notion, Henderson. All right go to it. You've absolute carte blanche to do as you think fit. And make this Press campaign a damned good one!'

So being a literary man of no mean skill Henderson immediately launched into his great newspaper campaign. The following morning all of Samuel T. Wernham's newspapers came out with similar headlines, but the most dominant one was: 'ARE OTHER EYES WATCHING US?'

Beneath this trenchant interrogation

there followed many columns putting forth the possibility of a super-scientific Eye and Ear, which could penetrate into the most secret places. To back up the theory there were mentioned the mystery of the atomic plant, the Walker case, and the peculiar instance of a certain famous financier, who was not identified by name, who had found himself black-mailed when one of his most secret 'conferences' had been bafflingly filmed in sound.

Inevitably Curtis, Christine and Dick read the newspapers and from them could easily see which way the wind was blowing, but still Curtis remained sitting tight.

'Yes, I agree they've made a gigantic stride,' he admitted, when Christine and Dick demanded to know what his next move would be. 'By some supreme jugglery of the mind which I cannot understand, this contributor — what's his name? — Michael Henderson, has acci-dentally hit the right nail on the head. But that doesn't mean that I've to be stampeded into a panic and rush out into the open declaring all I've done. I'm not going to do anything of the kind. I'm going to sit tight and wait and see what happens. Remember, I've got the Z-ray almost constantly on Scotland Yard, and they're the only ones that bother me. Up to now they're not in the slightest bit concerned, and as far as I can see they have no reason to be either. I'm just going to go on sitting tight and watch what Scotland Yard does next. You two can do as you please, just so long as you don't have any ideas about running away. Because the moment you do, you in particular, Christine, you know what'll happen to you. It pays you to keep silent just as much as it does me. Just behave yourselves and all will be well in the finish.'

Metropolitan Scotland Yard, however, were far more interested in the business than Curtis imagined. What Curtis did not know was that the interest of the police had reached as far as the chain of newspapers printing the fantastic supposition that other eyes were looking into the private lives of individuals. The most interested person of all was Chief Inspector Halliday, who was still worrying secretly over the Walker case, and the fact that Curtis had not so far received any of his reactions was because the Inspector had held most of his discussions at the newspaper offices, and not in his own office at Metropolitan Scotland Yard.

Indeed, even while Curtis was talking to Christine and Dick, Inspector Halliday was also talking to the chief news editor of the Wernham Press Syndicate. Since the syndicate operated under the name of the Zenith News Service, Halliday was not in the least aware of the famous financier's connection with the papers.

'I would be glad,' Halliday said, looking at the news editor across his broad desk, 'if you would call me the moment you get any particular information concerning this fantastic supposition envisaged by your writer Michael Henderson. Not that I expect you ever will get a reaction. But if you do the police would be interested just the same.'

'Because of the Walker case, I presume?' the news editor questioned.

'Exactly. There was something about that that was decidedly uncanny and I still haven't resolved it in my own mind. Since that time the two men whom we arrested have sworn again and again that no woman was anywhere near them at the time they made their arrangements. They have admitted that they unwittingly gave the name and address of the woman they were intending to murder, but their voices were kept low for obvious reasons. I've worked it all out, and I've even measured up the street where they held their discussion, and I'm perfectly convinced that no human agency could possibly have heard them. They also swear that they never mentioned the name or the address of their intended victim before. So no one could have known beforehand about this. I think your man Henderson has some very good ideas in that article of his, and I'm hoping it's just possible that it may bring into the open that mysterious woman who telephoned us. We won't feel the case is complete until we've got hold of her, for definitely she is an accessory, or at least, so we feel.'

'You think there might be a tie-up somewhere between the atomic plant, the Walker case and this financier, who seems to have been getting himself into some kind of trouble?'

'The financier doesn't interest us since he doesn't come into our particular orbit. But of course, Metropolitan Scotland Yard and M.I.5 are closely linked together and therefore the matter of the atomic plant and Annie Walker are somehow connected with a scientific device that can penetrate far beyond the range of the human eye and ear. Anyway,' Halliday smiled, getting to his feet, 'just let me know the moment you get any information, and we'll do the rest.'

'I will,' the news editor promised promptly, whose only concern was the dispensation of news and keeping on the right side of the law.

For the time being however a complete stalemate had fallen. Curtis Drew was absolutely determined to make no moves, and neither Dick nor Christine dared to make any. So the days drifted by, Curtis keeping a constant watch on the activities of Scotland Yard — via the Z-ray — in the hope that he would pick up some information which would guide him as to what was going to happen next. Inspector Halliday however, never mentioned anything of his private opinions whilst in his official headquarters — for the very simple reason that he had no desire to admit before his sergeant that he was having to rely upon the connivance of a chain of newspapers for the completion of a baffling case. It would cast too much reflection upon his high reputation. He was content to play a wait-and-see game in the hope that sooner or later something would turn up.

Meantime Michael Henderson kept up his series of articles in the hope that they would have an effect somewhere, but since he could not keep on doing the same three instances over and over again he had to fall back on scientific hypotheses and drag up examples of mysterious cases in the past, for which very reason his articles began to lose interest in the public favor and he was at his wit's end as to what he ought to do next.

And, back at his home, Curtis Drew sat tight and watched Scotland Yard. Till even upon him the strain began to tell — the strain of long days sitting before the televisor watching for something to happen via Scotland Yard. It was strange that never for a moment did it occur to him that Samuel T. Wernham might have something to do with the situation. Otherwise, had he tuned into that gentleman, he would probably have learned a good deal. However, he did not, and after nearly ten days of assiduous watching of the Yard and finding nothing that seemed to threaten his safety he finally gave up the surveillance and left the house one evening with the brief remark that he was going for exercise. The moment the door had closed Dick gave Christine a significant look.

'Are you thinking what I am thinking?' he asked. 'That we should do a bit more to add to our store of knowledge concerning the Z-ray?'

She nodded promptly. 'Definitely. This seems an excellent chance to clear up some of the final details about which we

211

are not so sure. Also, after such a long interval I've rather a hankering for setting that ray on the move again. Seeing if there is anything we can pick up. There is something so fascinating about the Eye that when you're away from it for a week or two — as we have been whilst Curt has been standing on guard so to speak — you miss it dreadfully.'

'Right,' Dick said, promptly, 'let's get on our way.'

They left the lounge quickly and hurried through to the laboratory. Here, realizing that time was more or less against them since they had no particular idea when Curtis would return, they went to work immediately adding to the store of details which they had already gathered concerning the Z-ray apparatus. This actually was Dick's job. Christine took little part in it but she did satisfy herself to the extent of switching the apparatus on and sending that mystery beam sweeping across the darkened country-side. Impelled by the old fascination she swept down upon city after city, maneuvering the beam now with the sureness of matured skill, and here and there she came to a halt and picked up the conversations of passers-by, most of it innocuous, indeed, even had it not been Christine had no intentions of cashing in on the unguarded remarks of other people. Meantime Dick went on making notes busily and correcting errors that had crept into his earlier drawings.

It was just as Christine was about to switch off that she suddenly paused, holding the Z-ray steady upon a point where there seemed to be standing an immense isolated building. In the upper rooms there were many lights and it seemed to be something in the nature of a hospital or an institution. Moving the beam closer Christine finally satisfied herself that the enormous edifice was indeed within its own grounds.

But it was not this particular fact that interested her. Her attention was centered upon a glowing redness at the base of this enormous building from which smoke, at present not very dense, was beginning to curl.

'Dick, quickly!' she exclaimed, turning

to him. 'Take a look at that! What do you imagine it is?'

Dick only needed to gaze for a few seconds before giving the answer.

'Fire! From the look of things that place is some kind of an institution and they're not aware that the basement is almost in flames. Whereabouts is it? What sort of a building is it supposed to be?'

Christine turned hurriedly to the projection map, which by the number system gave an exact location once the reading was made of the Z-ray's position.

'It's in a place called Woadbridge in Suffolk. About eighty miles away. Trouble is I don't know who they are or what kind of an institution it is so I can't ring them up.'

'No, but you can ring up the fire brigade or the police for that district,' Dick told her quickly. 'That whole lot is going to go up in flames if they don't get moving quickly.'

Christine did not waste any more time. She darted across to the telephone and whipped it up, quickly dialling for the operator.

'Number please?' came a voice.

'I don't know the number, but put me in touch with the police or the fire brigade at Woadbridge, Suffolk, right away please. Very urgent. A case of fire.'

'Fire?' repeated the voice of the operator in amazement. Then recovering herself: 'Woadbridge, fire brigade or police station. I'll put you in touch with the police right away. Your number please?'

'Riverbend 460,' Christine replied promptly. Then immediately she had done it she gave a little gasp to herself. She had given the number so naturally it had never occurred to her that in doing so she was giving a good deal away. However, the fact remained that there was a fire and many lives were in danger and by prompt action they could very probably be saved.

Then the voice of the sergeant at Woadbridge police headquarters came through.

'Yes, who's speaking please?'

'My name doesn't matter,' Christine said quickly. 'But there's a very large institution somewhere in your district which is at the moment catching fire. You'd better inform the necessary fire authorities immediately and you might be able to save it. The people in the building don't seem to be aware of the trouble.'

'Ah, that'll probably be the Old Pensioners' Home, ma'am. Where are you speaking from, please?'

'That doesn't signify. Just get busy quickly, and believe me this isn't a false alarm.'

With that Christine rang off and then stood biting her lip, giving Dick a troubled glance.

'Yes,' he said, grimly, 'I know what you're thinking. You gave the telephone number. Anyway, it's too late to retract it now, we'll just have to wait and see what happens.'

Christine nodded slowly, cursing herself for the fact that for the moment she had overlooked that in having to call the operator for a long-distance call it was essential that she give her own telephone number. This very fact seemed to her to be a situation loaded with dynamite.

In far away Woadbridge a police

sergeant was left scratching his head in some bewilderment, but nevertheless he did not waste another moment in sending out a call to the fire brigade. This prompt action, coupled with Christine's warning, was sufficient to catch the fire before it spread to the whole of the immense building housing old age pensioners. But in the small hours of the morning, when the danger was all over and the fire completely extinguished, the police sergeant was still a very much-puzzled man.

'What I don't get about that call,' he said to his colleague, as they sat in the dim light of their headquarters, and drank tea slowly, 'is that the woman said: 'somewhere in your district there's a big building'. I wonder what the devil she meant by that? I mean to say, why in your district? It would be in *her* district as well, wouldn't it?'

'I suppose so,' his colleague admitted. 'I can't see that it matters much anyway providing that we put the fire out.'

The sergeant, however, was a man who believed in thinking a little further, even though in this particular instance his concentrations did not get him very far.

'It just sounds,' he said, after a long interval, 'as though that woman was at a distance when she gave the warning. I'd say that she might have seen it from an aeroplane only in a case like that she couldn't have telephoned. If she was on the ground how the hell could she see the fire? And why did she contact the police first, and not the fire brigade if she's in the same district?'

'The only answer to that,' his colleague said, not very brightly, 'is that she's not in the same district.'

'Then how the blazes did she manage to see that there was a fire in the Institution?' The sergeant narrowed his eyes. 'Yes, there's something funny about this whole thing,' he continued, stroking his heavy chin. 'She said: 'there's a large institution . . . ' Well, surely, if she lived in this district she would know that the Old Age Pensioners' Building is the biggest thing there is around here? I don't get the hang of this thing at all. I think it's time somebody else knew about it.'

So the very much-puzzled sergeant

rang his colleague in the police department in the next nearest town, Ipswich. Since all police headquarters had been warned by Metropolitan Scotland Yard to be alert for any 'phone calls from an unknown woman, in connection with the still unsolved Walker case, it was not surprising that the Chief of the Ipswich Police Constabulary thought a good few things when this peculiar information came into his possession.

'It might not be anything — yet on the contrary it might be something.'

Thus it was that by morning Chief Inspector Halliday, in his office on the Thames Embankment, had all the information before him, and a very much-delighted man he was. Also at this time Curtis had returned to his usual constant watch over Scotland Yard, and for the first time in his long and tedious vigil he really got his teeth into some information. Listening and watching Curtis heard every word and saw every gesture of the Chief Inspector as he turned to the detective sergeant, busy at his own desk in the corner.

'There's something about this call to Woadbridge, Harry, that seems to link up,' he said, after a while. 'Of course, we never had any recording either optical or magnetic made of that unknown woman's voice when she 'phoned in about the Walker business, so we can't definitely say that the woman who rang Woadbridge last night was the same person. But there are certain parallels to be drawn. From the way the woman spoke it was absolutely beyond doubt that she was speaking from a distance. Otherwise, as the Woadbridge Inspector has pointed out, she would have known everything about Woadbridge itself. And since she did speak from a distance she would have been compelled to give the telephone exchange her own telephone number. It may have been a call box but it's worth an investigation.'

'I'll check back on that, sir, right away,' the sergeant said, getting to his feet. 'I can start with the London exchange and if it's passed through there they'll have a record of it. If that fails I'll try the others.'

Halliday nodded, lighted his pipe, then sat back to again study the various reports which had come in to him during the night. And on the edge of London Curtis Drew clenched his fists and waited tensely for what would happen next. It seemed as far as he could tell at the moment, that for the second time his 'darling sister' had been overcome by a sudden attack of generosity.

'If that proves to be right,' he breathed venomously, 'I'll finish her. Damned if I don't!'

It was half an hour before he got the information he wanted, which was when the detective-sergeant came to the end of his endeavors to trace the call. He gave a rather triumphant smile as he looked at his superior.

'The call was made from Riverbend 460, sir,' he said, 'and the time was nine-forty-two precisely.'

'And who's the subscriber to Riverbend 460?' the Inspector demanded.

'It's listed in the name of Curtis Drew, sir. Radio and television engineer.'

The Inspector's eyes narrowed. 'Oh, it is, is it? Radio and television engineer, eh? Does that seem to suggest something to you, sergeant?'

'It seems to suggest to me, sir, that there is somebody in that particular area who has the power to see and hear things at a distance. It doesn't appear to be Drew himself, because it's a woman's voice that speaks each time. Of course, that doesn't mean that Drew has nothing to do with it, but . . . '

'We've got all we need to know for the moment,' the Inspector said, 'and I think the best thing we can do is go out there and have a look right away.'

He got to his feet at the same moment as Curtis Drew got to his. Quivering with fury he switched off the instrument then rapidly went to work to unscrew the main panel. In a matter of ten minutes he had removed three of the most vital functioning parts of the apparatus and deliberately smashed them with a hammer till there was nothing left but a grounded mass of metal parts and broken glass. This debris he quickly took outside by the laboratory's rear door, buried it in the ground, and then returned once more into the laboratory. Without pausing he hurried through into the lounge where Dick and

Christine were just finishing a late breakfast.

'You can think yourself lucky,' Curtis said, malevolently striding across to where Christine was seated, 'that I don't kill you here and now, sis. During the night you used that Z-ray somehow — in spite of the fact that I thought I'd made it impossible to operate — and warned the police of Woadbridge about a fire! You gave the telephone number as well. Now Scotland Yard has got on to that and Scotland Yard is moving quick, and in this direction! I'm going! You two can do what the hell you like!'

With that he hesitated for a moment, his fists clenched, and it seemed for a moment as though he would actually strike Christine; then seeing Dick's dogged face as he jumped to his feet Curtis seemed to change his mind. He swung round and left the lounge hurriedly. Within five minutes he was departing again, a suitcase in his hand and the front door slammed behind him. The last glimpse Christine and Dick had of him was as he hurried out of the front gate and along the street.

'Now what happens?' Dick asked grimly. 'Do we clear out as well?'

'I see no earthly reason why we should,' Christine replied. 'There is nothing that we have done that can be considered wrong and I'm prepared to stand up for that no matter what happens. If the police come here we'll simply tell them the truth. That's all.'

It was not very long before Christine had the chance to implement her pledge. Within fifteen minutes a police car drew up outside the gate and from it there alighted Chief Inspector Halliday, the detective-sergeant, and a couple of plainclothes men. Christine herself opened the front door to them, and they followed her deferentially into the lounge.

'I'm here, madam, on a matter of extreme importance,' Halliday said, showing his warrant card. 'I am from the Metropolitan Police Headquarters and I wish to ask a few questions of a gentleman by the name of Curtis Drew.'

'Curtis Drew is my brother,' Christine said, quietly, 'but at the moment he's out of town. But do sit down, gentlemen, and I'll try and help you if I can.'

The men silently did as she requested. Then, after a moment's thought, Halliday continued:

'I was hoping to have a private interview with your brother, Miss Drew, but it is also more than possible that you could help our enquiry as well. Would I be right in thinking that last night you rang the police authorities at Woadbridge concerning a fire at an old pensioners' home?'

'Quite right,' Christine answered, simply.

The Inspector looked rather surprised at her ready acquiescence.

'You rang from here,' the Inspector continued. 'We have that fact definitely established. How could you conceivably know of a fire over eighty miles away?'

'I am not going to beat about the bush with this business Inspector, because both my fiancé here, Mr. Englefield, and myself are weary to death of the tyranny which we have undergone at the hands of my brother during the past few months. He invented what is known as the Z-ray, a television device by which it is possible to see and hear over thousands of miles without the need of a transmitter at the other end.'

'Ah!' the Inspector exclaimed, his eyes brightening. 'That fits everything into place so very concisely, Miss Drew. And since you are willing to be so frank I think I would be safe in assuming that it was you who rang up that night concerning the intended murder of Annie Walker?'

'Yes,' Christine admitted quietly. 'It was I.'

'And the matter of the Jetway Atomic Corporation?' the Inspector asked, slowly.

'I had nothing whatever to do with that. It was my brother's affair entirely. I don't even know what arrangements he made, what plans he photographed through the Z-ray, or anything at all about it.'

'You do testify to the fact, though, that it was he who was responsible for the disappearance of that information from the Atomic Corporation?'

'Most certainly I do. Mr. Englefield here can confirm it.'

'And you say that your brother is out of town at the moment?'

'I imagine he will get out of town as quickly as possible,' Christine responded. 'Since I have told you so much, Inspector, I may as well tell you more. My brother had his Z-ray constantly tuned upon Metropolitan Scotland Yard in order that he might know in advance if any moves were going to be made against him. Earlier on today you evidently made arrangements to come here, and of course he was forewarned of the fact and promptly took his departure. Where he is now I haven't the slightest idea, but of course I think it a reasonable assumption that he will not return.'

'You are amazingly frank about all this,' Halliday said, thinking. 'The only explanation for it can be that you have suffered so much at the hands of your brother you are more than willing to give the information that we desire. I think you should know, Miss Drew, that up to now I have been fully of the opinion that you were connected with the attempted murder of Annie Walker and I have made most exhaustive endeavours to trace you after that 'phone call.'

'Yes, I know of those endeavours,' Christine smiled. 'The Z-ray told us everything. But I give you my assurance that I do not know Annie Walker, and that I had no connection with the two men who were plotting to kill her. I happened to have the Z-ray upon them when they were discussing the murder so I promptly gave the warning which — I was glad to note — saved Annie Walker's life. That is the whole truth.'

'And I'm willing to confirm every word she has said,' Dick remarked. 'But you're certainly going to have to move mighty fast if you're going to catch up with Curtis, Inspector. I don't doubt that he's got everything prepared for a quick get-away, right out of the country, I mean.'

The Inspector nodded slowly and then asked, 'Have you seen the pictures in the newspapers lately purporting to be a fair portraiture of one Henry Brixton?'

'I have, yes,' Christine admitted, 'and Brixton is, of course, my brother. He was involved in some dubious deal with Samuel T. Wernham, the financier, and the stories which were printed about the supposed Brixton were undoubtedly the beginning of my brother's downfall.'

'In that case,' the Inspector said, glancing at the sergeant at his side, 'you'd better advise headquarters, Harry, to have all railway stations and airports watched for a person answering to the description of Henry Brixton whose picture recently appeared in the Press. Contact the newspapers concerned and tell them to let us have a reproduction photograph immediately for distribution to all police officials. The moment Brixton, alias Curtis Drew, is picked up I am to be notified immediately.'

'Right, sir,' the sergeant assented, getting to his feet. He went out into the hall.

'There is another matter, also, on which you might be able to throw some light, Miss Drew,' the Inspector continued, seeming more at his ease now. 'Recently there was a case of apparent suicide concerning a man named Herbert

Sandhurst. I said 'apparent suicide' because when the police were asked to investigate the matter I took charge of the case and found within Sandhurst's car quite a number of fingerprints, which did not tally with Sandhurst's own. There was nobody whom we could openly accuse of murder — and indeed, we were not sure whether it was murder — or as it appeared to be, a suicide. But in the course of my investigations into Sandhurst's past life I did discover that one of his biggest enemies was a radio engineer by the name of Curtis Drew. There were also several others, but Curtis Drew figured amongst them.

'Finding that information didn't do me any particular good at the time, of course, and later our pathologist proved that Sandhurst had indeed taken his own life. But I would like to have interviewed the man or the person — for it could have been a woman as I thought then — who had been present with Sandhurst in his car . . . That person might have been able to throw light on his suicide, which seemed to be connected with an obvious murder of another man who was an enemy of Sandhurst's. I trust, Miss Drew, that I'm not making this sound too complicated?'

'No, I can gather what you mean,' Christine replied with a faint smile. 'The man Sandhurst you are referring to was a person whom my brother referred to as Mr. B. And the man whom you found murdered my brother always called Mr. A. To cut matters short he set those two men at each other's throats and B. murdered A. Afterwards B. killed himself. My brother came upon him in his car, for he was intending to blackmail him — and all unwittingly my brother left fingerprints behind.'

'Very interesting,' the Inspector mused. 'It was only this morning when I realized that the name of your brother was Curtis Drew that I remembered his connection with Sandhurst. It would appear from that then that he incited to murder and indeed brought that murder about as well as being the cause of a suicide?'

'That I'm afraid is true,' Christine admitted, sighing.

'Altogether,' the Inspector said grimly, 'your brother has quite a deal to answer for, and we shall spare no pains to have him picked up. Meantime, as a matter of verification, these two gentlemen here — ' he nodded to the plain-clothes men ' — are from our 'backroom' department. Would it be possible for me to see this Z-ray apparatus of which you have spoken?'

'Certainly,' Christine assented, rising to her feet. 'Come this way, gentlemen.'

She led the way into the laboratory and then stood aside with Dick close beside her whilst the experts went to work to study the equipment. Altogether it took them half-an-hour, the Chief Inspector hardly speaking in the interval, then at last one of the technicians turned and shrugged.

'There seems to be little doubt, Inspector, that this instrument is all that Miss Drew claims for it, but several of the vital parts have been destroyed.'

'They have?' Christine raised her eyebrows. 'That's just about what Curt would do! Since he's not able to use the apparatus himself any more he's done his best to make sure that nobody else can! But in that he is not altogether correct. Mr. Englefield and I between us and at different times, noted down all the details of this apparatus for the simple reason that we had the hope later, when we had escaped my brother's clutches, that we might build a similar instrument and turn it solely to beneficial uses — such as warning of approaching murder or fire; incidents similar to those which have already come to your notice, Inspector.'

'Does this mean,' the Inspector asked quickly, 'that you have enough details for this machine to be rebuilt by experts?'

'I see no reason why not,' Christine responded. 'Get the plans and details from your room, Dick, and let the Inspector see them.'

Dick nodded and hurried out. In a few moments he was back and handed the bulky mass of notes and drawings to the Inspector. He shook his head and motioned to the engineers at his side. They took the papers and began to study them.

'Well?' The Inspector asked presently.

'Little doubt about it,' one of the men replied. 'With all these details we could very easily put the apparatus in order again. Indeed there's enough information here to build a separate apparatus altogether.'

'That,' Halliday said slowly, 'is just what I was hoping. You know, I have the feeling that Drew, having invented such a marvelous contrivance, will not be willing to let it lie here and do nothing. For obvious reasons he will not be able to build another for he will know that the police will have a watch over his bank account and, unless he gets money from another source, he will not have enough finance to start building anything new. Further, if he bought the special equipment and components that are needed for this machine he would immediately be traced. No, I don't think he'll try and build a new one — but I do think that if he's left in peace he might try and return to this one and even perhaps make an effort to remove a good deal of it to some quiet location where he can start all over again. It is perfectly obvious to me that your brother is a man hardly lacking in assurance, Miss Drew.'

'Lacking?' Christine echoed hollowly. 'The trouble is he's got too much of it! That's what all the worry has been about. If he had more sense and caution he wouldn't be in this mess now!'

'Do you, as his sister, think he's the kind of man who might return to try and use this apparatus or else remove the parts of it which are most vital and reconstruct it somewhere else?'

'I should think it is highly possible,' Christine acceded.

'That,' the Chief Inspector said, with a taut smile, 'is all I want to know. This apparatus will be left here exactly as it is, and you and Mr. Englefield will be taken into police custody for the time being.'

'So you're going to arrest me after all, and him?' Christine asked seriously.

'You're not being arrested, Miss Drew; neither are you, Mr. Englefield. This is a matter of police protection. I want both of you out of the way and I'll spread a story into the papers that will make it appear that you have been arrested. I'm going to try and lay a bait for Curtis Drew and if I am anything of a student of psychology I think that he may bite.'

★ ★ ★

That same evening the news of the arrest of Christine Drew and Dick Englefield hit the headlines. Not a great deal of information was given concerning the Z-ray but it was definitely stated that both of them had been charged with the violation of public privacy together with a lot of other high-sounding indictments which to the public in general made little sense. The only thing that Mr. and Mrs. John Citizen could hang on to was the fact that the Jetway Corporation mystery had been solved along with the riddle of Annie Walker.

Three people in separate parts of the Metropolis were particularly interested in the news — they were Samuel T. Wernham, Michael Henderson and Curtis Drew himself. Curtis had not fled the country: he was still within the city itself which he considered a far safer place to get lost in than by making a deliberate dash to a sea or airport. The more he studied the news the more he grinned.

'So they got the works and I'm left sitting pretty,' he mused, reading the information in the newsroom of a public library. 'Best thing I can do is lie low for a few weeks until the heat is off then I'll think what to do next.'

Samuel T. Wernham's reaction on the other hand was to immediately call Henderson to his home and question him.

'What move are you going to make next, Henderson?' Samuel T. demanded. 'Remember, I don't want Curtis Drew himself, or Henry Brixton, or whatever he calls himself. What I want is the secret of his invention! If you can find any possible way of contacting him I'm still willing to pay that two-million to get the secret. There doesn't seem to be any reference that the mysterious apparatus that has been used has been removed from the place where it has been operated, and according to the telephone directory the address is 27, Riverbend Terrace, North West 10. Somehow you've got to get hold of Drew. The police, just as I thought they would, have nailed the wrong culprits, or at least I think so. I can't see that Christine Drew and young Englefield, who both look like a couple of schoolchildren according to their photographs, could plan anything worthwhile. It's Drew himself who must have done all the dirty work, and it's him I want to contact. It surprises me that the police have been so stupid as to pin everything on these two young people and yet don't seem very worried as to what's happened to Drew himself.'

'It is possible,' Henderson replied, 'that the police believe that Christine Drew is the main person responsible. Remember that it was a woman's voice that did the talking on the telephone and the police have a habit of letting their minds run in grooves. They've been looking for a woman — and they've found one who exactly fits the whole case. The possibility is that they won't look any further.'

'Anyway,' Samuel T. said irritably, 'that's beside the point. What I want to know is, how are you going to find Drew?'

'I'm not going to try and find him,' Henderson replied calmly. 'I'm going to let him come to me.'

'You sound as though you really believe that!'

'I do, sir, for I look at it this way: The apparatus which Drew has been using could give him the complete mastery of the world, and he knows it. For the moment he has obviously had to abandon it, but can you see a man of his ambition just letting things go like that? He has only two choices. Either to build a new one which will be an almost impossible feat when for obvious reasons he will have to lie low; or else use the one he's already got. Just as a mother will brave all dangers to get to her child in an emergency, so I think a man with an immensely valuable apparatus, which will put him on top of the world, will also brave everything to get it under his control. Does that sound logical?'

'More or less,' the tycoon admitted. 'So

what do you intend doing?'

'I intend to keep a constant watch on 27 Riverbend Terrace in the hope that sooner or later Curtis Drew will return. I'll investigate the place tonight and make sure that there's no police watch over it: if there isn't it makes my job all the easier. If there is I shall have to use various strategies. I feel quite convinced that sooner or later Drew will come back when he thinks that all is safe. Of course, for that matter,' Henderson continued, 'the police may be playing a similar game. You are inclined to regard them as fools, sir, but I never have. They know exactly what they're doing and they move very ingeniously to gain their point. Anyhow, whatever they do my plan remains unchanged. I am going to wait for Drew. Because obviously to try and find him would be an absolute impossibility.'

'Just as you wish,' Samuel T. responded, 'it's up to you. Notify me the minute you do find him or better still bring him straight to me by the shortest possible route.'

Henderson had made his plans and he carried them out. That night he made a careful investigation of 27 Riverbend Terrace, and he admitted to himself that he was surprised to find that dwelling was deserted and completely in darkness with no trace of any police supervision anywhere. It was not that Henderson missed any police signs for he was too big an expert in such matters: he satisfied himself that there definitely were no police present anywhere.

Since the house was detached and the neighbors some little distance off he had no difficulty in finding his way into the laboratory at the rear of the residence and here he satisfied himself that the apparatus which Samuel T. Wernham so badly wanted was still in position. Whether it was still operative or not Henderson did not know, nor did he attempt to find out. One glance satisfied him that the apparatus could not be moved without a great deal of commotion and that would be the last thing that Samuel T. Wernham would want. Open, barehanded stealing was not in his line. So with tireless patience Henderson set himself to wait, and when necessity forced him from his watchdog efforts another man of equal tenacity took his place. Day and night there was a watch on 27 Riverbend Terrace.

And the police waited too — and so did Christine and Dick Englefield.

The newspapers and other media were told to play down the whole business and within two days all mention of the Jetway Atomic Corporation affair had disappeared. Hidden in a small rooming house in the depths of London Curtis was aware that the hue and cry was disappearing but he still waited and watched warily. But inevitably his mind was drawn back to the Z-ray and the colossal possibilities he had thrown overboard in making his dash to safety. The more he thought about it the more infuriated he became until at last that reckless streak in his nature got the better of him.

Knowing the apparatus so intimately he knew that it was most unlikely that the authorities had moved it away. If they required to experiment with it at all — which he did not see how they could with the vital parts removed — they would have to do it from the laboratory itself. So he began to move and in various directions eyes sharpened to see if he would walk into the trap.

He did. His first awareness of it was when — fourteen days after his disappearance — he reappeared on an exceptionally dark evening and after a careful study of his surroundings he cautiously entered his laboratory with his own latchkey. Carefully drawing the shades he looked about him on the old familiar surroundings. The place was dank and cold and still. But the stillness did not last. There was a footstep.

He turned sharply and found himself looking at a small-built man with a placid face and a tired smile. In one hand he held an automatic steadily.

'Who the devil are you?' Drew blazed at him.

'The name is Michael Henderson,' the newcomer explained calmly. 'I'm rather hoping that you will remember my recent articles concerning you, Mr. Drew, or should I say Mr. Brixton?'

Curtis' gaze lowered to the automatic

and Henderson's smile widened slightly.

'You need have no fear, Mr. Drew; I am not going to use this upon you. It is merely a precaution. Nor am I acting of my own volition. I wish you to come with me to see Mr. Samuel T. Wernham. I believe you have already made the gentleman's acquaintance before. I think he has a proposition to discuss with you.'

Drew hesitated and looked about him at which Henderson cocked his automatic more suggestively.

'I would not advise delay, Mr. Drew, if you please. I have a car quite close at hand.'

'Very well,' Drew said abruptly.

With that he turned and left the laboratory again, locking it after him. After which he went ahead of Henderson as he held the automatic steadily to make sure there were no false moves. In silence both men got in the car, Henderson steering with one hand, still keeping the automatic ready with the other. Since his car was one of the automatic de-clutching variety this presented no difficulty to him.

Of necessity their journey to Samuel T.

Wernham's residence took them through the center of the city but long before they had reached the magnate's home they found their way blocked by a mysterious convergence of three police cars.

'What the devil's the idea of this?' Drew demanded angrily. 'I thought you said you were from Wernham? You're nothing more or less than a blasted cop!'

'I am no cop,' Henderson replied, looking worriedly outside. 'This development is something for which I am not at all prepared, Mr. Drew. I have the feeling that both of us are liable to get into difficulties — and quickly!'

His assumption was correct. The doors of the car were thrown open and burly police officers stood outside.

'You're under arrest, both of you,' one of them said, 'Get out of that car!'

'On what authority?' Drew demanded.

'On the authority that you are Curtis Drew and that the man with you is Michael Henderson. You are both wanted at police headquarters. There is a patrol car waiting to take you so hurry up!'

'I'll do nothing of the kind.' Drew retorted.

'You have no possible way of knowing the identity of either of us nor upon what mission we are engaged, so I . . . '

'You can save your breath, Mr. Drew,' the big uniformed officer replied. 'I am Detective-Sergeant Crespin, Chief Inspector Halliday's right-hand man. I can cut a long story short and save you a lot of grief by explaining that the Z-ray that you recently invented has been turned against you. Your entire apparatus has been reconstructed at Scotland Yard from plans and specifications made by your sister and her fiancé, and ever since the instrument has been completed a few days ago we have kept constant watch for the moment when you would return to your laboratory. The guess turned out right and you did return. A most practical demonstration of the Z-ray since it has also roped in Mr. Henderson here, whom we have been wanting to contact with regard to various matters for quite a long time.'

Drew breathed hard but he didn't say anything. He scrambled out into the street.

'A pity,' the Detective-Sergeant said with a wry smile, 'that your own Z-ray had to be used to finally locate you. Mr. Drew. You see, once we picked you up on your return to the laboratory you would then never have been able to escape us. Wherever you might have gone on this Earth we would have found you, but that won't be necessary now. The car's over there. Walk quickly, if you please . . . '

THE END

CLIMATE INCORPORATED
THE FIVE MATCHBOXES
EXCEPT FOR ONE THING
BLACK MARIA, M.A.
ONE STEP TOO FAR
THE THIRTY-FIRST OF JUNE
THE FROZEN LIMIT
ONE REMAINED SEATED
THE MURDERED SCHOOLGIRL
SECRET OF THE RING
OTHER EYES WATCHING